A VAMPIRE QUEEN'S DIARY BOOK 3

DEATH'S DELIVERER

BY

P. A. HARRELL

AKNOWLEDGEMENTS

I would like to thank my loving husband Randy for this wonderful life or death depending on how you look at it. Oh how you make my heart sing with joy! I would like to thank my three best friends Lisa, Marylou and Lissa, for standing by me while I was composing my diary. Ladies you are the best friends a vampire queen could every ask for. I would also like to thank all of my family and friends who have stood by me through thick and thin making this third book possible. I love you all!

Table of Contents

PROLOGUE

As I soaked in the tub, I closed my eyes and saw within my mind's eye the times I had rested my head against my beloved's chest and felt him begin to wash me. The tears began to flow down my cheeks. Oh how I missed his touch! I rose from the tub, dried myself, went to our lonely bed and cried myself to sleep. As with every night since I had lost him, I dreamed. I watched in horror as the bullet hit him and the virus took him. I woke screaming his name. I laid there shivering in the bed. He had always been there to soothe me after the nightmares. But after his loss the nightmares were never ending.

CHAPTER 1

A TIME OF GREAT SORROW

It had been five years since I lost the love of my life to the darkness. I had prayed to our god, every night since that horrible day, to keep him save. I had a special place constructed to house his body, as the darkness did not destroy it. He laid there as if asleep. The sorrow and grief had overwhelmed me so much over the years I had became cold. I no longer cared about any human hunter or the fact they were innocents. Their kind took from me the one thing I loved the most. So every night I went in search of the hunters. Making them pay for taking him from me. I would not rest until I had rid our world of their kind! As I stared down at those beautiful green eyes the tears began to fall down my face. I whispered in the cold silence, "Oh, my love, how I miss you! Never feeling your loving arms around me. Never feeling your wonderful lips upon mine. But I promise you, I will never stop hunting for the madmen who have taken you away from me. Some day I will kill them all and avenge your death!" I bent down and kissed him tenderly on the lips. I left heading into the night in search of the hunters. I was out stalking one night, hunting for my prey. As I ran through the forest, I no longer felt anything for the beautiful night. The only thing I could feel was the hatred that had engulfed my heart. I no longer enjoyed the run or the chase. I still took out the evils, for I had to feed, but the fun of the chase was no longer there. It had been about an hour since I had left home. I had already fed, so I was in search of hunters. I came upon an encampment. There were three men gathered around the campfire. I knew those men were hunters by the weapons they carried. I sat high above them on a tree branch. The fire in my heart was building. I began to see red! The hatred exploded inside me. I leaped to the ground, taking out the first man, breaking his neck. I then went after the other two. One of them reached for his bow and readied himself to fire. But over those last five years I had became quite skilled at eluding the arrow. He fired at me. I shot straight up into the sky and the arrow missed. I swooped back down and broke his neck before he could reload the bow. The third man had taken to the forest. I leaped back into the sky and began to track him. I scented him while I was in the camp, so he was very easy to follow. I spotted him in a clearing. He was running as fast as he could, trying to reach where they had parked a car. It did no good, I was too fast for him. I landed right in front of him, startling him. He stumbled backwards, trying to get away from me. I leaped at him, knocking him to the ground, looked down at him and said, "Well hunter, that was quite fun, but it is time to die!" He looked up at me and said, "You are the vampire warrior queen who is seeking out our kind, because we took your king from you, aren't you?" I smiled at him and said, "That I am. I am queen Anne, wife to king Camaz, of Mexico, a mighty vampire warrior who your kind took from me. I am sworn to take all hunters lives for taking that of my one true love!" I proceeded to rip his throat out. A few hours later, when I had returned home, I went down to our quarters. I undressed from my hunting attire and walked naked into the bathroom to run a hot bath. As I soaked in the tub, I closed my eyes and saw within my mind's eye, the times I had rested my head against my beloved's chest and felt him begin to wash me. The tears began to flow down my cheeks. Oh how I missed his touch! I then rose from the tub, dried myself, and went to my lonely bed, crying myself to sleep. As with every night since I lost him, I dreamed. I watched in horror as the bullet hit him and the virus took him. I woke up screaming his name. I laid there shivering in the bed. He had always been there to soothe me after the nightmares. But after his death, the nightmares were never ending. It had now been ten years since that awful day. I had rid our country of all vampire hunters. None would enter from the outside for they feared me. In their world I was called, Death's Deliverer. Every night before I hunted I went to where my beloved was laid to rest. I talked to him, telling him how much I loved and missed him. As the blood tears ran down my face I heard a voice in my head. It was Cassandra calling to me. I closed my eyes and pulled

into my mind. She appeared to me and said, "I am so sorry you

suffer so, my dear. Do you remember when you died? I told you I

would send you back to Earth with special gifts?" I looked at her

and said, "Yes, but so far only one has manifested itself." "There is

another, my child. You have the ability to bring him back!" With a

look of bewilderment I said, "What?" "Yes, you have the ability to

bring him back. But it is very dangerous, for you must enter the

darkness to save him. That involves taking a mortal wound. You

must be strong and fight the darkness, keeping it from taking you

as well. Your journey to find and save your beloved will then

begin. In order for it to work you must inflict the wound yourself."

I said to her, "I will do anything to have my true love back with

me!" "Then go lie down beside him and do what you must!" Then

she is gone. I opened my eyes and looked upon my husband and

said, "I am coming my love. We will be together soon!" I laid

down beside of him, pulled one of my daggers from its sleeve and raised it to my throat, cutting deeply. I felt my blood begin to flow down my neck. I began to slip into the darkness as my blood left my body. I had not cut deep enough to end my life. Soon I was floating in the darkness. I knew I must find him quickly or I would die from blood loss. I began to scream out his name and listened for a response. It was hard to move around in the darkness, but I let my hearing range out for any sound of Camaz. I didn't know how long I had been in the darkness, but it felt like years. I was so lonely! I called out to him again and again. Then I heard a faint call way off in the darkness! Could this have been my true love? I began to scream out his name over and over. I followed the sound. I was getting closer and closer. Then I heard him! He was calling my name over and over. I followed the sound. It was so black there I couldn't see a thing, but I knew he was close. Then I heard his sweet voice whispering to me, "My one true love, you have found me! I am so sorry I left you, but the darkness took me. There was nothing I could do." "Oh, Camaz, I am so glad I have found you!

But we do not have much time. I am dying! I need you to wake up, please wake up!" I felt myself slipping deeper into the darkness. Oh god, I was going to die! "Please, please wake up, my love!" Suddenly I felt a pull, but it was not the darkness. I felt our blood bond pulling at my heart. I began to fight the darkness with all that was in me. Then I felt the fire ignite in my throat. The scorching fire jolted me. I opened my eyes and looked into his beautiful emerald green eyes. I went to reach for him, but I was to weak. He tenderly lifted me and said, "Oh how I have yearned to have you in my arms again!" He turned his head saying, "Drink, my love, you are still very weak. Come back to me, my beautiful queen!" I opened my mouth and bit down, his sweet blood began to flow into my mouth. I could already feel my strength returning. After a few minutes, I released my hold on his neck and pulled him to my lips. I kissed him tenderly as my heart sang with joy. He picked me up, caring me down to our quarters. He laid me on our bed staring down at me with a longing I had not seen in many years. He asked, "How long was I gone?" The tears began to flow down my cheeks and I answered, "My love, it has been ten years since that horrible day, but I never gave up on us, for I knew our love was eternal!" He pulled me to him hugging me to his chest telling me how much he loved me and how brave I had been. He laid me down on the bed, stroking my face. I smiled him and said, "Oh, how I have longed for this day! I need you so badly!" He began to kiss me, igniting a fire within me I had never felt before. I screamed out his name as he took me. That night he made love to me like there was no tomorrow. Afterward I fell off to sleep in my loving husband's arms. The following evening we went up to let everyone know the good news. Our daughter came running up leaping into her father's arms. He hugged her close and said, "Hello, my beautiful daughter. How I have missed you!" "Oh, father, I still cannot believe you have returned to us!" He set her down and walked over to Camazotz. I could see the tears in our son's eyes. He hugged his father to him and said, "Welcome back Father you have been missed greatly!" After everyone had said their hellos, we all sat down and I told them how I had entered the darkness and found him. After about an hour we returned to our quarters to dress for the hunt. I could hardly wait to run with my beloved again. While we were dressing he asked me about the hunters. I told him, "I have rid our country of all hunters over the last 10 years and none will enter our lands because of me. They call me Death's Deliverer!" He chuckled and said, "That's my girl!" He pulled me to him hugging me to his chest.

CHAPTER 2

OH, TO LIE IN THE SUN AGAIN

A few days later, while we were hunting, I told Camaz I longed to lie in the sun again. He smiled at me and said, "If that is your wish then I shall fulfill it!" Suddenly I caught the scent of our prey. I smiled at him and leaped into the air. He followed close behind. I began to breath in the wonderful smell, letting my nose guide me. Soon we were deep in the city. We landed on top of a building, perched there and scented the air for our prey. I looked down at the silent street below and saw two men standing on a corner. The evil rolling off of them was setting my throat on fire. We watched as two street walkers approached the men. They began to talk. I could tell those men were not interested, they were looking for good women to rape and murder. They sent the women on their way. I smiled at Camaz and took to the air. We followed the men as they walked down the street looking for their next victim. Little did they know they were on the menu that night. We swooped down picking them up and carried them into the sky. They began to scream, but no one could hear them. We were soon over the woods. We landed in an open area. I was in the mood for a chase. so I released my catch and said, "Now we are going to play a little game of hide and seek. I will give you a five minute head start. Then I am going to hunt you down and kill you! So go!" Camaz had released his prey as well. They both took off running into the woods. The excitement of the chase was building within me. I could hardly hold myself back. But I did, I had promised him a five minute head start, so I waited. A few minutes later Camaz asked me, "Well, my dear, are you ready for the chase?" "I was born ready!" So off we ran like the wind, into the forest. Soon we were deep in the woods. We leaped into a tree and scented the air for our prey. I picked them up and thought, "Oh goodie, they are both together." We took flight going after them. Soon we spotted them, they had stopped to catch their breath. We landed a few feet away from them. The look on their faces was priceless! My prey began to run off to the west, Camaz's to the east. I took off running. God, how I loved to run! Within seconds I caught up with him and leaped, knocking him to the ground. I looked down at him and said, "Game over!" I pushed his head to the side and struck. His wonderfully evil blood began to flow. I lapped up every drop. I could hear Camaz calling to me. He had caught and finished his dinner and was on his way to me. As I sat there waiting for his return, I looked up at the night sky. I thought to myself, "Oh, how I have missed this beautiful sight!" Camaz landed in front of me, and helped me to my feet. He pulled me into his arms telling me how much he loved me. The following evening, when we woke, he told me all had been arraigned for our trip and we would be leaving for our island in a few hours. I could hardly wait for sunrise so I could feel the sun upon my face! We went hunting first so we would not have to leave the island that night. As we sped toward the island, I enjoyed the wind in my hair and the smell of the salt air. It was close to daybreak when we arrived, so we hurried into the house and unpacked everything. We strip naked and walked out onto the sand. We stood there holding each other as the sun rose. I felt the wonderful warmth on my skin and tingle of the change coming. I turned to Camaz and smiled. He was glowing pale red. He took me in his arms and said, "Oh how I have longed to see my beautiful queen again in the sunlight again!" He began to kiss me. We tumbled to the sand. As I laid there on my back he stared down at me smiling the whole time. We made love on the beach for hours. I screamed his name over and over. Then we just laid there enjoying the sun. As the sun began to set we went inside to ready ourselves to go to the mainland to hunt. A few days later, as we walked hand in hand on the beach, I looked up at him and said, "My love, I have something to tell you." "What is that, my dear?" "I am with child again!" Before I knew it he had scooped me up into his arms and was kissing me madly. He broke the kiss saying, "Oh, my one true love, you have made me the happiest vampire in the world, for the second time! How far along are you?" I smiled at him and said, "Just a little over a week, my love." He said, "We must make ready to get you back home!" I said, "Can we stay another week please? I so love being in the sun!" "If that is your wish, then we shall stay!" For the next week we laid on the beach during the day and at night. Camaz went to the mainland to hunt and brought back y meals. God, how I loved takeout food! At the end of the week we made ready to leave our island. Oh, how I was going to miss being in the sun. But he wanted me back home safe. We arrived at the castle around 4am. Everyone was getting ready for their sleep of death. We would not tell them the good news until the following evening. So we said our good nights and retired to our quarters. I was sitting at my dressing table brushing my hair when Camaz came up to me and took the brush. I loved when he brushed my hair! He pulled my hair to one side and kissed my neck. He picked me up, carrying me to our bed. He laid me down. I looked up at him and said, "You do not have to carry me my king, I can walk." He smiled at me and said, "I know, but I do it because I love the feel of you in my arms!" He kissed me tenderly. I fell to sleep with a big smile on my face. That night I dreamed., but it was a good dream. I dreamed of our child. It was a beautiful little girl with my creamy white completion and Camaz's beautiful emerald eyes. Her hair was the color of corn silk. As I stared into her beautiful eyes, she smiled up at me. From that moment she stole my heart! The next evening when we woke I told Camaz of the wonderful dream of our child. He smiled at me and said, "I hope she is as beautiful and as gentle a soul as you, my queen!" I said, "It was just a dream, it doesn't mean it will be a girl. We may have another son." "My dear, your dreams have always been true. So I will await our daughter." I smiled at him and kissed him tenderly. It was the beginning of my fourth week, I had grown heavy with our child. I could feel the pull beginning. Our child's birth would be soon. I told Camaz we needed to move to the third floor to prepare for the birth. He had everything made ready and we had moved up to the birthing quarters. I had just finish my meal when I felt the pull become very strong. I felt the joy engulf my body as our child made ready to meet the world. I could hardly wait to look upon her, or his, face. But then something happened. I began to feel strange. Then a great pain took me. I began to scream. Camaz was at my side in seconds asking, "What is wrong, my love?" "Oh Camaz, something is wrong! I have a horrible pain in my stomach. It feels like something is trying to rip our child from my womb!" Tears were streaking down my face as the pain became unbearable. I began to scream and shriek his name. Camaz had summoned the healers and they were in the room with us. I heard them tell Camaz the child had not turned and was sideways in in the birth canal and we were both going to die! I heard him scream out, "NO! There must be something we can do! I will not lose both of them!" I could feel the darkness pulling at me. I screamed out to him, "Camaz please, please, help me the darkness is coming. Please do not let it take the child and me!" I heard the healer tell Camaz there might be a way but is was very dangerous. Camaz had to take the child from my belly. Almost like preforming a C-section but instead of a scalpel he would have to use his teeth. He came over to me and said, "Do you understand what I must do, dear?" I looked at him. With pain in my voice and answered, "Do what you must, but please do not let the darkness take me. If it does, I will never be able to come back. Cassandra told me, when she sent me back to you so long ago, there would not be a second chance!" The darkness was beginning to surround me. I could feel it's pull. It was telling me to give in, that I would feel the pain no more! But I fought it with all of my might. Suddenly I felt a sharp pain in my stomach, then ripping. I screamed out in agony. But the pain had chased the darkness away. So I was happy to endure the horrible pain. I screamed out to him, "Camaz, it is working the pain is chasing the darkness away, but hurry I do not know how much longer it will stay away!" Then I felt a different pain, more intense than the last.

It felt as though the child was being ripped from my body. Then it stopped, I laid there pain free. I opened my eyes. My tears had soaked the bed. I looked into my loving husband's face. It was blood smeared. He smiled at me and said, "Thank god, I thought I had lost you!" He was cradling our child in his arms. He laid the child on my chest and said, "Behold, our daughter. The child of your dreams." I looked into her face and she was as I pictured her in the dream. She had hair the color of corn silk, my completion and Camaz's emerald green eyes. She smiled up at me and I began to cry tears of joy. Camaz took the baby, letting me know the healers must take care of me. When they finished, we were told there was so much damage done that I would never be able to conceive again. My heart broke with those words but Camaz said, "It is alright my love, I do not need anymore children. Your have given me all a man could ask for. Our daughter and son!" He pulled me to his lips, kissing me tenderly. My heart sang for him. I was so happy we had survived the ordeal and still had our beautiful daughter. I looked into her beautiful face and proclaimed. "I shall call you Jade and you will be loved as no other!" Afterward, Camazotz came into the room to meet his new baby sister. He smiled at me and said, "Oh mother, she is so beautiful!" I smiled at him and said, "As you were, my son. You are both my heart!" He kissed me on my cheek and whispered, "I love you!" "As I love you, my son!" After everyone had left our quarters, Camaz came over and sat down beside of me and said, "You scared the hell out of me, woman! I thought I had lost you forever! Never put me through that again!" I looked at him with sad eyes and said, "I am sorry, my love, but as the darkness began to take me, all I could think of was being without you. I fought with all of my being to keep it from taking me!" He pulled me up into his arms, kissing me tenderly.

CHAPTER 3

PRINCESS JADE

Over the next three years Jade grew into a stunning young woman. Her corn silk hair hung down to her waist in waves. Her beautiful eyes were deep emerald green, like her father's. Her speed and agility amazed me. She was even faster than her father. I was busy in our quarters planning her coming of age party. Over the years we had learned she, like us, could walk in the sun. We had purchased an island off the coast of Greece for her gift. We planned on taking her there after the party to surprise her. It was three days later and everyone had started arriving for her party. We had taken her to Paris the month before to find a gown for the party. I watched as she slipped into the beautiful dress. It was a pale pink with pearls on the top. She looked so lovely in the dress! I had chosen a gown a few shades darker than hers. I went to her, kissed her on the cheek and told her how beautiful she looked. I handed her a wooden box. She smiled at me and opened the box. Inside was a tiara with pink and white diamonds, a necklace, earrings and bracelets that matched. She smiled and said, "Oh, Mother, they are so beautiful! I love them!" I smiled at her and said, "I am glad you like them, my daughter, your Father and I picked them out for you when we where in Paris." There came a knock on her door. Jade said, "Come in Father." He walked in and smiled at our daughter and said, "My little princess, you look stunning!" "Thank you Father." He looked at me and said, "My dear, as always you take my breath away!" I smiled at him and said, "I love you too, my one true love!" He gave me a quick kiss and turned to our daughter, "Are you ready my dear?" "Yes Father, I am." We left her room, Camaz had me on one arm and Jade on the other, walking his two favorite girls down to the party. We entered the great hall. Everyone stood up and cheered. He walked us to our table, pulled the chair out for me, then escorted our daughter to stand before the council. The ceremony began and Astor proclaimed her an adult. She walked to the table where all her friends where. They all congratulated here. Afterward she came to sit at our table. Camaz called the party to order and toasted our daughter on reaching womanhood. As I watched her go to the dance floor with one of her friends, I sighed. Camaz looked at me and asked, "What is wrong, my love?" "Our baby is all grown up and I will never again feel the joy of having another child. This saddens me, my love." "My wife, we have four beautiful children, much more than I had ever dreamed possible. I still remember the day you had asked me about fathering an heir. At that time I had not even considered it, for I thought it was not possible. But now as I gaze upon all our children my heart sings! Thank you!" He made my heart soar! I bent and kissed him tenderly, saying, "I love you! Thank you for this wondrous life you have given me and all of our beautiful children!" He smiled at me, I could see the pride in his eyes. I was his and he was mine for all of eternity. After the party, we returned to our quarters to ready ourselves for the hunt. He took me into his arms and asked, "Are you happy, my queen?" "Oh yes, very much so.

I am so glad you chose me back in 1974. You have made me the happiest woman on earth!" He kissed me tenderly and said, "Come, let us enjoy all this wonderful night has to offer, my love." A few minutes later we were air borne searching for our prey. We reached a small clearing in the woods and sat down. I let my sense of smell fan out, searching for the wonderful smell of evil. Camaz alerted me he had picked up on something. We began to follow the scent. A few miles in, we came upon a campsite. There was a man, woman and three small children there. They all smelled of the innocence. We could still smell the scent of evil. Then a man appeared from one of the tents. The delicious smell was rolling off of him. He was with those people and seamed to be family. He began to play with the children. They were laughing and having a good time. I pointed up to the tree beside of us and we both leaped to the top. We were high enough for them not to hear us. "What shall we do, my love? He seams to be family to those people. How will we get him away from them?" I'm not sure, but let us continue to hunt, we will come back later." So we took to the air again. Soon I picked up a scent off to the east. We began to follow it until we reached town. We landed atop a radio tower to test the air for the direction of the wonderful scent. Camaz quickly picked it up and we took off in the direction of it's origin. We landed on a dark street and came upon the house where the sent was originating. Suddenly I picked up on another scent, that of a vampire. We leaped to the top of a building and watched as the vampire came into view. It was a woman. She was quite beautiful. She was of Mexican descent. She had long black hair and dark brown eyes. Camaz proclaimed, "I know this woman." I looked at him and asked, "Who is she?" "Her name is Candice, she is one of Louisa's college friends." He told me to stay put as he did not want to frighten her. He leaped to the ground. I watched as he approached her. I had readied myself just in case there was a problem. I watched as they began to talk. She hugged him and said hello. I felt the ugly head of jealousy rise in me. I thought to myself, "Stop it!

He has no interest in this woman other than her being a friend of Louisa!" I watched as Camaz told her of me, he signaled for me to come down. I leaped from the ledge and landed beside them. Camaz announced, "Anne, I would like to introduce you to Candice, she is an old friend of my sister." I smiled and responded, "Hello Candice. I am very pleased to met you." She smiled at me and said, "The pleasure is all mine, lady Anne. I am so happy Camaz finally found someone to love. He had been alone for so long." We talked for a little while longer and said our goodbyes. We took to the air and started searching for other prey, leaving the one there for her. As we were hunting for dinner he asked, "What is wrong, beloved, you seem distant?" "I am okay, just thinking about the hunt." I hated lying to him, but I couldn't let him know I was jealous of the woman. Suddenly I caught a whiff of the man we had seen earlier, at the campsite. He was alone and seemed to be searching for someone. I pointed to where the man was and we dropped down a few feet from where he was. His blood was was calling to me, setting my throat ablaze. I began to stalk him. The closer I got the more intense the burn became. Then I had an idea. I removed my clothes and ran toward the man screaming for help. He stopped me and asked, "What is wrong? Are you okay?" "No, I was attacked by a madman. He is chasing me, please help me!" Then Camaz entered the area. I screamed, "That's him! Please do not let him take me again!" I cowered behind the man. God I loved the game. The man yelled at Camaz, "Hey, what did you do to this woman? You have her scared to death!" Camaz walked up to the man. The stranger pulled a knife and took a protective stance saying, "Stay back or I will cut you!" Camaz began to laugh and said, "My good man, I cannot scare her to death. She is already dead!" I knocked him to the ground. He looked up at me and said, "What the hell? Why did you do that?" I smiled at him, baring my fangs and said, "Because I am quite hungry and have tired of this game!" I leaped on him, he tried to cut me with his knife but I knocked it from his hand. I slammed his head to the side and struck. His blood began to flow, igniting the blood lust in me. I drank him down quickly, stood, wiping the blood from my mouth and said, "That was quite fun. Are you ready for another game of it, my love?" "Yes, as a mater of fact, I am starving!" We took to the air to search for his meal. A few hours later we arrived back at the castle. The children had all returned from their hunt and were getting ready for sleep. We said our good nights and headed for our quarters. Once behind closed doors Camaz pulled me to him, kissing me passionately. I felt the burn began way down low. My body cried out for him. He broke our kiss and asked, "Shall we take a shower first, my love?" I smiled at him and said, "That would be wonderful. I love when you wash my body, it makes me so hot!" He picked me up carrying me into the bathroom. He got the shower ready and we entered. I stood under the hot water enjoying its warmth. He picked up the sponge and began to wash me. As he washed my back I felt his lips on my shoulder. He whispered, "My god woman, you are so beautiful. You sent my soul on fire!" I turned to face him and looked at his beautiful body glistening in the water and said, "Do you have any idea how hot you make me just talking to me that way?" He pulled me to him and began kissing me. I felt the heat between my legs bursting into flames. I moaned in his mouth, "My need is great, my love!" He reached around me grasping my buttocks and lifted me onto his manhood. I felt as he entered me and I screamed out his name with each thrust. The entire time he was kissing my neck because he knew the thrill it gave me. He licked the base of my neck then nibbled it, sending me over the edge! I screamed out in ecstasy, digging my nails into his back and I bit him, causing him to explode. He stood holding me, still buried deep inside of me. Our bodies were racked with our climax. He began to remove himself, every so slowly. I threw my head back and my eyes roll back. God, the man was amazing! A few minutes later we were in our bed awaiting sleep. He pulled me to his chest and said, "Woman, you never cease to amaze me! That was the most I have ever heard you scream! You were so hot and wet inside. It was as if you were still human!" "You set my soul ablaze, my love. I have never felt such passion in all of my life! Oh, how I love you!" "You are my heart. I would gladly lay down my life for you! You please me in all ways possible, my queen!" He kissed me tenderly and we fell to sleep in each others arms. The following evening, when we arose Jade was waiting for us. She had some news for us. She had been accepted to Harvard. I said, "Wow, our little girl a Harvard woman." We congratulated her and let her know we would begin planning for her trip in a few days. Camaz met with our lawyers and had a house purchased for her so she would have her privacy. She signed up for night classes and would be starting in the fall. I was so happy for our little girl, but also sad as she would be leaving home. But I had to let her go, she was a grown woman.

CHAPTER 4

SUPRISE FOR KIMSU

One evening we received word Astor needed to speak with us. We entered the council chamber and Astor said, "We have received word from afar, a creature resembling Kimsu has been spotted in Japan. From the description, it is possible it is his kind. But that is all we know." I smiled and said, "Then we will travel to Japan to seek out this creature. We owe it to Kimsu to find his kind." We left the council's chamber and headed to our room to get ready to hunt. While I was dressing, I ask, "Do you think it is possible they have found someone of Kimsu's kind, my love?" "I do not know, but I think we owe it to him to find out." "I don't think we should tell him until we know for sure. I would hate to see him get his hopes up and it not be true." "You have such a good heart, my queen!" We left the in search of our meal. The following evening we were making plans for the trip to Japan. Kimsu walked into the room and asked, "What are you two up to?" I smiled and said, "Not much, just planing out next vacation. How are you this evening, Kimsu?" "I am quite fine my lady and you?" "Getting a little hungry, would you like to accompany us on the hunt?" He smiled and said, "I would love to. I am in the mood for a good chase!" "Me also. Oh, how I love a good chase!" We made plans to meet up, a little later, for the hunt. A few hours later we were sitting atop a building testing the air for our prey. Kimsu had transformed into fox form. I was still amazed at his beauty. He was standing next to me. I reached over and stroked his silky fur. He smiled at me, showing all of those razor sharp teeth. I said, "You are a good and true friend, Kimsu. I am proud to call you my friend." He licked the back of my hand, his tongue was rough, like that of a cat. All of a sudden he lifted his head and sniffed the air. He had caught a whiff of something. He leaped to the ground and began to stalk his prey. I had also caught the scent. There were five in all. I knew the scents immediately. they were hunters! I screamed to Kimsu, "Look out! They are vampire hunters!" I said to Camaz, "How dare they enter our lands! I will tear them to pieces!" I leaped to the ground with Camaz following. We caught up to Kimsu and went after the hunters. I could still remember how my heart broke when they took Camaz, my one true love, from me. The anger was rapidly building in me. A few minutes later we were just outside of town. We spotted their campfire and headed toward it. I listened as the men were making plans to attack our home. I grew even more pissed! I leaped high into a tree overlooking their camp. Camaz and Kimsu stayed on the ground and were circling around on both sides of the encampment. Once they were in place, I leaped from the tree and landed in the camp. The look on the men faces were priceless. One man went for his bow but was knocked to the ground by Kimsu. Who quickly ripped out the man's throat out. Another man yelled, "Who the hell are you?" I replied, "I am Death's Deliverer, here to take all of your lives!" I leaped at the man, knocking him to the ground. As I sat on him I said, "How dare you enter my lands! Now you shall pay with your life!" I felt something sharp strike my shoulder. I screamed out in pain as the arrow dug deep. I rolled off the man, but not before I broke his neck. I laid there shrieking as the silver began to burn. But I knew I had to get up or they would get me. I looked to my left then my right. Both Camaz and Kimsu were in battle with the hunters. The third hunter was coming for me. I quickly jumped to my feet and unsheathed my sword. He had a bow and the arrow was ready for release. I watched as the arrow left the bow, heading straight for me. As I said earlier, I had become quite skilled at defeating hunters. I swung my sword just as the arrow reached me, knocking it to the ground. He reached for another arrow and prepared to let it fly. I ran at him, with lightning speed, taking him down before he could release the arrow. I said, "For all the evil you have done to my people, I take your life for my own pleasure." I swung my sword downward, removing his head. I looked around to make sure there were no other hunters. I reached up and yanked the arrow from my shoulder. I screamed from the pain and fell back onto the soft grass. I stared at the beautiful night sky. Then I heard Camaz's voice, "My one true love, are you alright? Did the arrow strike your chest?" I smiled, "No my love, only in my shoulder. I have already removed the arrow." He reached for me, helping me to my feet. Then surveyed the damage the arrow had caused. "It is a nasty wound, but it will heal. Come lets leave this place and get you back to the castle." He lifted me into his arms and leaped into the sky, flying me back home. When we arrived, he took me down to our chambers. He laid me on the bed and opened his wrist allowing his blood to flow into the wound. I felt the wound begin to heal. He told me he was going to the holding cells for my meal. While he was gone I thought to myself, "If these hunters were brave enough to enter our lands, then there could be more of them! We would need to start a search of our lands the following night. Camaz returned with my meal. I quickly drained the man. I could already feel my strength returning

I told Camaz of my plan to search for other hunters. He said, "Do you really think there could be more of them, my love?" "Yes, they are like rats. When they invade a land, they are everywhere. It took me almost 10 years to rid our country of their kind and now they are back!" "Then we will start our search tomorrow and will not rest until we have eradicated them from our lands." "Yes, I will make them remember why I am called Death's Deliverer!" He pulled me to his lips, kissing me tenderly. "My mighty warrior queen. Oh how proud you make me! Now sleep, my love and get well." He began to sing to me. God, how I loved to hear him sing! Slowly I drifted off to sleep. The following evening we arose and dressed in our battle gear. We would have to put off our trip to Japan, as we had much more important things at hand. We gathered all of our elite, family and friends to scour the countryside for the vermin. We would not rest until all of them were destroyed! While we were out searching, we came upon a group of hunters in the woods. As we neared I stopped dead in my tracks. I could not believe what I was seeing. They had ghouls with them! Fear took hold of me and I began to tremble. Camaz was quickly at my side telling me everything was going to be alright. But I knew what those creatures were capable of, especially being with the hunters. The group could be deadly! I told Camaz, "We must be very careful. We must surprise them. If they know we are coming, they will be ready for us. Let us take to the trees so the ghouls cannot smell us." We leaped into the trees, staring down on there camp. I counted a total of twenty hunters and fifteen ghouls. We were going to need help! Over the last few months I had learned Kimsu's beast language. I called out to him letting him know he needed to go for reinforcements. All the hunters and ghouls heard was the howls of foxes, so they paid no attention to us. I watched as Kimsu took off to alert the others. I looked into my husband's eyes, asking, "What shall we do, we cannot take them all on by ourselves? Maybe the hunters, but not the ghouls!" "We shall stay here until the others arrive. But if they begin to leave, we must attack!" So we sat in the tree watching them very closely. Suddenly two of the men got up and said they were going into town for supplies. We watched as they left the encampment. I smiled at Camaz and took to the air. He followed right behind me. The two would not get far. They reached their car and sped off. We followed until they were a few miles away from their friends, then landed in front of the car, causing the driver to swerve and end up in a ditch. We removed them from the car dragging them toward the woods. They were screaming, but no one could hear them. I slammed my captive into a tree with such force I knocked him out. Camaz had his captive by the throat. I watched as he broke the man's neck like a twig. He dropped the lifeless body to the ground. My captive came to, looked up at me and said, "Please don't hurt me. I have done nothing to you!" I smiled down at him, showing my fangs. I watched the fear build in his eyes, then said, "You do not deserve to live after what you and your kind where planing to do to us." I picked him up in front of me, my hands around his neck and jerked his head, snapping his neck. I dropped his body to the ground. We headed back to the encampment to wait for the others. We were back in the tree looking down on all the hunters' group. I did not fear the hunters, but I feared the ghouls. I knew what their bite could cause. Just I heard Kimsu's howl letting me know they were on the way. I looked at Camaz and said, "They are coming, we must get ready!" "My dear, I want you to do something for me." "What?" "I want you to stay here in the safety of the trees." "No! I will not stay behind while you risk your life! I am not afraid of them!" I leaped to the ground with my sword drawn. He landed beside me. We charged the group. I could hear the others coming, so I went for the first two ghouls in front of me. Taking their heads as I attacked. Camaz was in battle with a ghoul and a hunter. He was moving so quickly it was hard to keep up with him. I heard a noise behind me. I turned with my sword made ready. There was a ghoul in front of me. He smiled exposing all of those razor sharp teeth and said, "My, my! Isn't this my lucky day? I have Death's Deliverer in front of me!" He then charged me. I sidestepped him and raked my sword across his chest. He screamed in pain and ran at me again. I swung around again but misjudged my steps, he slammed into me, knocking me backwards. I hit the ground so hard I lost my sword and he was coming for me! I pulled my daggers from their sleeves and made ready for his attack. He leapt on me knocking one of my daggers from my hand. I pulled my knees up into his chest to keep him off me, but he was pushing his head closer and closer. I thought to myself, "Shit, got to do something or he is going to bite me!" I broke my arm holding the dagger free and slammed it into his chest. It was not a mortal wound, but it gave me enough time to roll and sling him off me. Then I took off running to where my sword lay. He was right on my heels as he leapt, knocking me face own in the dirt. I was just inches from my sword and reached for it. I rose up with the ghoul still on my back and slammed him against the nearest tree. He released his hold and I turned, swung my sword and removed his head. I stood there briefly and then ran into the heat of the battle. There were many hunters and ghouls dead on the ground. I watched as Kimsu stalked one of the hunters, backing him into a tree. I watched him gracefully leap at the man and rip his throat out. I looked around for Camaz finding him in the heat of battle with two ghouls. They had him on the ground and he was fighting for his life. I watched as one of the ghouls prepared to bite him. I screamed at the top of my lungs running toward the ghoul. I swung my sword and severing his head from his shoulders. It startled the other ghoul enough to allow Camaz the opportunity to bring his daggers around, stabbing both deep into the ghoul's heart.

I ran to Camaz and said, "Baby, please, please tell me you have not been bitten!" He smiled at me and said, "No, my dear, I have not been bitten." I reached for him, helping him to his feet. We took off to help the others. By the time we were done, all of the hunters and ghouls had been defeated. Thank our god none of our warriors have been bitten or killed! We gather our wounded and headed back to the castle. Leaving the wounded with the healers, we left to search for more hunters. After a thorough search, no more hunters or ghouls were found. We had rid our lands of the vermin once more!

CHAPTER 5

KIMSU'S MATE

A few weeks after the battle with the hunters we were in Japan searching for Kimsu's kind. We started in Tokyo were our Intel said the creature had been spotted. We were staying with friends of Camaz, Akatsuki and Kimiko, at the outskirts of town. They told us the last sighting of the beast occurred not far. As we were out hunting for it, I scented the air to see if I could pick up a smell similar to Kimsu, but all I could smell was the sweet blood of the innocent. We ventured farther out in our search. Soon I caught a whiff of something pure evil. It set my throat ablaze. I was quite hungry so I let the others know I had picked up on dinner, afterward we would continue our search. I dropped into my hunting crouch and began stalking our prey. We soon came upon a house. The smell was strong all around the house. I had detected at least four inside. I crept up to a window and looked inside. There were three men and one woman. All smelled of evil. I signaled the others to come forward, but suddenly I picked up another scent. It was one I had not smelled before, but there was something alarming about it. I instantly turned around just in time to see a streak of silver go by. I heard a howl. I knew the howl and understood it! It was a Night Kitsune and female. I returned her howl. She came from the shadows looking for the one calling her. But she only seen me. She began to growl, stalking me. I held up my hand then in her language I explain what I was. I watched as she shifted into human form. My god, she was beautiful! She had long jet black hair and big beautiful brown eyes. I could tell she was of Japanese origins. Then she spoke, "How do you know my language? You are not like me." I smiled, "No, I am not like you, but I know of one who is. He is my best friend, Kimsu." She gave me an odd look and said, "Impossible! I have lived over 200 years and have never come in contact with another of my kind, I am the last!" I invited for her to return with us to met Kimsu. She agreed, but said, "I must go now. I am quite hungry." I said, "You do not have to leave. We, like you, hunt the evils. There is plenty to go around. Please join us?" Camaz and our friends landed beside us. I introduced my new friend, Chiyo, her name meant eternal. We proceed to go after our prey. Once inside the house, Chiyo changed back to her fox form. I watched as she approached her prey in the living room. I heard the woman scream out as Chiyo leaped on her. But the screaming stopped, for Chiyo had ripped out her throat. Chiyo began devouring her meal. Two of the men rush into the room. They saw Chiyo and me. I smiled at them, baring my fangs. The fear in their faces made my blood boil and my killing instincts take over. I leaped on one of the men, knocking him to the ground. I was so thirsty I couldn't take the time to play with him. I slammed his head to the side and stuck. The other man rushed me. He had a knife. He pulled my head back and prepared to slit my throat. But before he could stike, Camaz was all over him. Camaz yanked him from me, slamming him into the wall. I heard his skull crack from the impact. Camaz yelled at the man, "How dare you lay your hands on my wife? I will tear you limb from limb!" I watched as he did just that! He approached me and asked, "Are you alright, my dear? Did he cut you?" "No, I am fine, but I though he was going to get me. Thank you, my love!" He helped me to my feet. We went to make sure all four were dead, then we left the house. We invited Chiyo to join us at the house and she agreed. A few days later we said goodbye to our friends and headed for the airport. Chiyo came with us. I could hardly wait for Kimsu to meet her. We arrived home around 2am. I looked for Kimsu but was told he was hunting. I took Chiyo to the guest quarters. She had changed back into human form. She looked to be about my size, so I went to my closest and selected one of my evening dresses. I brought it to her and she tried it on. It fit her perfectly. We went downstairs to await Kimsu's return. Camaz had gone to talk to Astor so we were alone in the living room. Camazotz, our son, entered the room. He hugged and welcomed me home. I introduced him to Chiyo. He instantly knew there was something 'off' about her. Being best friends with Kimsu, he knew the scent. He proclaimed, "She is like Kimsu! I can tell by her scent. Oh mother, I am so happy you found someone, he is so lonely!" We all talked for a bit then Camazotz excuses himself as he was going hunting. That was when Kimsu walked into the room. I watched as their eyes met. He smiled the most beautiful smile. I introduced them. They both had shifted into their fox forms. I watched as Kimsu approached her. He turned, encircling her with his tails. She did the same. I listened as they howled their joy. Then, instantly, they were back in human form. Kimsu came to me, hugging me to him and said, "Oh, thank you, Lady Anne! You have made my heart sing with joy! We are soulmates, as you and Camaz are!" "Oh, Kimsu, I am so happy for you both! I hope you have a very long and happy life together. That is all I have ever wanted for you, my dear friend!" They shifted back to fox form and ran into the beautiful night. A few minutes later my love walked into the room. I said,

"Oh Camaz, they are soul mates like us! I am so happy we found her!" He pulled me to him, staring into my eyes and said "I am so pleased for them, dear. I knew it would all work out." He pulled me to his lips, kissing me with all that was in him. I felt the fire began to build way down low and I groaned. He broke our kiss and said, "Oh my, I so love when you make that sound!" He pulled me into his arms and carried me down to our quarters. As soon as we were in the room, I began ripping at his clothes until I had him completely naked. He proceeded to remove my clothing. We stood there staring at each other, I could see his lust for me building. He picked me up, carrying me to the bed. He laid me down. Slowly, he began kissing down my neck. My slow burn to turn into an inferno. I pulled him to my lips, kissing him passionately. I breathed into his mouth, saying, "My need is urgent, my love. My body aches for you!" I felt him enter me. I screamed out in ecstasy, my eyes rolling back in my head as the climax took me. I lifted my hips to him with each thrust. He kissed my neck and worked his way down to the base of my throat. There he began to lick, driving me over the edge! I began to buck beneath him, digging my nails into his back, leaving long bleeding streaks. He then flipped me over, pulling me to him. Taking me from behind he went deep and I felt him hit my sweet spot. I exploded from the ecstasy, screaming his name over and over. He began to move faster and faster until he released himself. It was then he bit into my neck and began lapping at the blood. We collapsed panting wildly. He rolled to his side, propped up on one elbow. Smiled he said, "My god, woman, you are amazing! Oh, how I love to hear you scream my name over and over, knowing what pleasure I am giving you!" "I love every minute you are inside of me. But when you bite me, that's what sets my soul on fire. As when you bit me the first time so many years ago!" "Oh, my queen, how I love you!" He pulled me to his chest and a few minutes later I was fast asleep. That night I dreamed of happy times. The first time I met him. When he took me as his own. My introduction to the council. Our children and our endless nights of love making. It was such a beautiful dream! Then it changed. I saw Kimsu and Chiyo running through the woods happily. I saw their cubs three of them, two boys and a girl. I was so happy for my friends! Then I heard our god whisper to me, "Anne, I am so pleased you are so very happy. But I have come to warn you. Happiness will not last much longer. I have seen great change coming in your relationship with Camaz. Beware, there will come a woman from afar who will compete for his attention. He has known this woman in the past and they were together for awhile. You must fight with all within you to hold his heart!" I woke abruptly, tears flowing down my cheeks. Camaz pulled me to him asking, "What is wrong, my love, have you had another bad dream?" I didn't tell him of Cassandra's warning, but let him think it was just a nightmare. He held me in his arms telling me everything would be alright. But I knew what was coming and I had to prepare myself for it. A few days later my nightmare turned into reality. We had just returned from a hunting trip when we were greeted by Astor. He told Camaz he had something to discuss with him. I told him to go ahead I was going to change. When I entered our chambers I began to have a very uneasy feeling. My radar was going off left and right. Something or someone was coming. By the look on Astor's face, it was not good news. I sat down on the bed, closed my eyes and withdrew into myself. I opened my mind and linked to Camaz. Then I was inside his head looking out at Astor. I hated doing that because Camaz didn't know I was with him. I listened to their conversation. Astor began, "Sire, I have some very disturbing news. I have just received word Josefina has returned to our lands." I heard Camaz gasp and say, "Where and when?" "She is staying at her friend Juanita's, just out side of town. She has asked to see you." I was totally shocked when Camaz replied, "Anne must not know of this! I will go to Josefina and ask her to leave." He got up and said goodbye to Astor. I could tell he was heading back to our room, so I quickly slip out of his mind. A few minutes later he walked into the room.

I was sitting at my dressing table brushing my hair. He came over, taking the brush from me and began to brush my hair. My heart was aching knowing what I had just learned, but I had to be very careful. Cassandra had warned me of what was coming. He sensed the distress in me and asked, "What is wrong, my love, you seem to be worrying about something?" I answered, "I don't know, my love, I just have a very bad feeling something is going to happen to us!" "Never! I will not allow anything to happen to you, my dear. I will guard you with my life!" He kissed me tenderly. As we were getting ready for bed I said, "Camaz, what would you do if something did happen to me? Would you find another to make you happy?" He looked at me strange and said, "Where is this coming from? Nothing is going to happen to you, I promise. If I were to ever lose you, there could be no other. You are my soul mate and one true love!" I began to cry. As the tears ran down my face he wiped them away saying, "My queen, it breaks my heart to see you so unhappy, come here." He took me in his arms, telling me he had loved me from the first time he saw me and would love me for all

of eternity. The next evening when we arose, he let me know he

had to go into town on business. But would return in a few hours

and we would go hunting. I waited about thirty minutes after he

left and began to track him. I had to see the woman and what his

reaction was going to be. I hated the ugly head of my jealousy had

risen, but I had to know. I trusted Camaz, but I didn't trust the

woman. I stayed back far enough so he didn't pick up on my scent.

I soon arrived at the house were he had gone. I watched as he

knocked on the door. A woman answered and invited him in. I

heard her call to Josefina, letting her know she had a visitor. I went

up on the porch and looked through a window. I saw a tall, light

skinned woman with long, black hair and hazel eyes. She was very

beautiful and refined. I felt the anger begin to rise in me. How dare

she go after my man! I watched as Camaz entered the room. She

ran up to him and hugged him, telling him how much she had

missed him. I watched as he pushed her away from him and said,

"Josefina, you left me long ago. You chose not to be with me. I no longer have feelings for you. So I have come to ask you to leave." I watched as she began to work him. She came up to him and said, "I know I did wrong by leaving you, my love, but I have learned from my mistake and I have come to ask for your forgiveness. I want you to take me back!" That really pissed me off. How dare her try and take him from me, I began to see red. But then I heard him say, "Josefina, that is not possible. I no longer have those feelings for you. I have found my one true love and soul mate. We have been a mated couple for over 40 years. She is the only woman that makes my heart sing! So please leave, you are not wanted here." His words made my heart soar. I was so happy. I had been so afraid he would chose her over me! All of a sudden she was on him. She began to kiss him but he broke the kiss telling her, "No, it will do you no good to try and seduce me. My woman puts you to shame!" He turned, heading for the door. As I leapt into the air I heard her scream, "No, you will be mine! I will have you!" Oh

how I had wanted to go back and rip her throat out, but I could not.
Camaz could not find out I knew. I hurried back home, beating him
by just minutes. I sat on our bed and pretended to be reading one of
my books when Camaz entered the room. I looked up at him and
smiled, he said, "Well, my dear, are you ready to go hunting?"
"Yes, my love, I am famished!" I could still hear Josephina's words
echoing in my head. But if she came anywhere near him I would
kill her! We left the castle around three a.m. I had decided to run. It
would help me take my mind off of Josephina. I stopped, sniff the
air and picked up on a scent. I pointed off to the west. We took off
running like the wind. Soon we came upon two men and one
woman. She was an innocent. The men had abducted her from her
home and planned on raping and killing her. We stalked them to
their campsite. There, we saw one more man. The evil was rolling
off of him. He was the ring leader. They took the woman over to
him and shoved her down in front of him. I could hear the woman
crying and begging for her life. The ring leader told her to shut up

and kicked her. She screamed out in pain. He grabbed her by the hair dragging her into the tent. I had had enough! The hatred for the man was like a red hot poker in my chest. I leapt from my hiding spot and ran full force at the two men still outside. I snapped the neck of the first and took the other to the ground. Camaz had landing beside of us. I looked up and said, "Here my love, this one is yours. I am going after the other one!" I leapt to my feet, ran to the tent and entered. The leader had the woman on the ground and was getting ready to rape her. I screamed, "Get off of her, asshole! What don't you come give me a try?" He jumped up from the woman and ran at me. Just as he reached me, I reached out grabbing both of his arms. I then pulled, ripping them from his body. He began to scream. I threw his arms to the side and leapt on him. I slammed his head to the side. I ripped his throat out with my teeth. I lapped up his wonderfully evil blood. I looked toward the woman and saw the horror on her face. I stopped feeding and wiped my mouth on my arm and said, "I am sorry you had to see that, my dear. Do not worry, I will make it so you do not remember." She asked, "Are you a vampire?" "Yes, my dear, that I am. My kind are not like the vampires of your myths. We only take the blood of very evil humans. You are a innocent, so you have nothing to fear from me." I caught her with my eyes saying, "You will not remember anything that has happen here tonight. You will tell anyone who asks that when you came to they were all dead. Do you understand?" "Yes." "Good, I will leave you now." I left the tent and leapt into the air with Camaz right behind me. He asked, "Are you alright, my dear?" "Yes, I am fine. It just sets my soul on fire to see one human being being so cruel to another!" We arrived back home a few minutes later. Maria greeted us at the door telling us we had a visitor waiting for us in the living room. We thanked her and went in. I froze in my tracks. It was Josefina! How dare she come to our home! I was so angry, but I had to be careful, remembering Cassandra's warning. Camaz said, "Josefina, what are you doing here!" She smiled and said, "I have come to plead with you, again. I want you to take me back." That really pissed me off. I said, "Camaz, who is this woman and what is she talking about?" He looked at me with shame in his eyes and said, "This is Josefina. We were once lovers, but that was a long time ago. I am sorry I did not tell you. She is who I went to see earlier. I ask her to leave, but she has not listened to me." I looked toward her and said, "You are not welcome in our home, please leave!" She laughed, "This is who you chose over me? A made vampire? What can she offer you? She cannot even give you children as I can!" I had had enough! "Listen here bitch, Camaz is my husband and you are wrong, for I have given him two children already. You have no stake in him. He belongs to me body and soul! Now, I suggest you leave our home or I will make you leave!" "I would like to see you try! I am over 900 years old and was born not bitten. I am much stronger than you. I challenge you to a fight to the death. This is my right as a royal!" I thought to myself, "Oh goodie, the bitch is going to die by my hand!" I answered, "I accept your challenge!

Name the place and time, I will be there!" She replied, "Tomorrow evening in the arena!" She then left our house. Now I knew what Cassandra meant when she said I would have to fight for him. That bitch was in for the surprise of her life! They did not call me 'Death's Deliverer' for nothing! Once we were in our room he took me in his arms and said, "My dear, you do not have to do this!" I answered, "Oh, but I do. She is trying to take you from me. I will fight anyone who tries, for as I said, you are mine!" He pulled me to his lips, kissing me passionately. We made love for hours that night with him telling me, over and over how much he loved me. I fell asleep with a smile on my face.

CHAPTER 6

BATTLE CRIES

The next evening when I woke I went down to the holding cells and drained two captives quickly. I wanted to make sure I was ready for the bitch! My sword was behind my back and my daggers were on my arms. I was ready to do battle for my one true love. Camaz told me Josefina was a mighty warrior in her own right, but I was much better than she. I walked out into the arena., She was there waiting for me. The council announced the challenge had been made and accepted and would be a battle to the death. I drew my sword and said, "Come and get some!" She charged me. I swung my sword, catching her across the arm. She screamed in pain and turned to face me. She said, "I am going to kill you and he will be mine, as it should be!" "Please, even if you could beat me, he would never give you the time of day!" She ran, screaming, at me. With a swing of her sword, she caught me across the chest.

The wound was not deep but it really pissed me off. I began to circle her, getting closer and closer. I leapt at her, knocking her to the ground. She lost her sword, but went for her daggers. I said, "Oh no you don't." I grabbed one of my daggers and plunged it into the hand reaching for her dagger. She screamed in pain. I raised my sword for the killing blow and said, "It is my right to take your life for trying to take my man from me. But I will give you a choice, something I'm sure you would not have given me. I will let you live if you agree to leave our lands and never return. Shall it be that or death?" "I cannot live without him, so I choose death!" She replied "Then so be it!" I brought my sword down and removed her head. Deep down inside I was hoping she would chose death. I stood up from her body, raise my sword to my husband and said, "You are mine as I am yours. Let no other come between us or let them suffer the same fate!" He leapt down to me, took me in his arms and said, "My mighty warrior queen, there can never be another. You are my heart, my love, my life." He kissed me tenderly. He life!" Then he kissed me tenderly. He picked me up, caring me out of the arena. We never spoke of that night again. A few months later we were planning a trip back to the Congo. We heard from friends that there had been unexplained killings. They had not been able to identify the creature doing the killing. We had been asked to help. While we were getting our gear together I asked, "What do you think this creature could be, my love? How is it no one has even scented it?" "I do not know my dear, all I know is it is killing innocents and we cannot allow it to continue." A few hours later we were aboard our plane heading for the mighty Congo. I had picked up the third installment of the books I had been reading, about a girl who fell in love with a vampire. I must say, the author was quite good. I had enjoyed every one of her books so far. Soon I began to feel the pull of sleep. It was calling to me. I closed my book and went to our bed. Camaz was already there, waiting for me. He pulled me him, kissed me tenderly and said, "I love you!" "As I love you!" I laid my head on his chest and he stroked my hair. I fell into blissfully sleep. Later we were jolted awake by the feel of the plane touching down. We quickly dressed in our battle gear and disembarked the plane. An hour later we were deep in the jungle. We met up with our friends and were hunting the mysterious creature. From what we were told, all of the victims were savagely torn to pieces. Suddenly we heard someone cry out. We ran toward the screaming. We stopped dead in our tracks, for there, in front of us, was a beast. It had the body of a man, but what looked like the face of a hyena. I said,,"What the hell is that!" Our friend, JoJo, replied, "That is a Hyena man. The legends say they are deadly ravenous creatures." I said, "My god! It has two mouths!" "Yes, they have one for eating and one for talking. They are also shape shifters." I said, "We must stop him before he kills the man! But how do you battle such a beast? How do we stop it? There must be a way." He replied, "According to legend, to catch one we must lay down a beautiful naked woman who will lustfully captivate the Hyena Man. He will, at that moment be vulnerable to attack."

Camaz smiled at me and said, "I have just the beautiful woman for the job!" I laughed and said, "Flattery will get you everywhere my love." But he was right. I had to do it to save the innocents. I stripped naked in front of them and Camaz said, "Any man or creature that does not lust for her beautiful face and body is stupid!" I smiled at him and said, "Thank you, my love." I slowly walked toward the Hyena man. He looked up from the man he had pinned on the ground. I saw lust began to build in his glowing yellow eyes. I laid down in front of him. He stared at me and said with one of his mouths, "My god, you are beautiful! Are you offering yourself to me, goddess?" I replied, "Only if you let the man go. Then you shall have me." He turned to the man saying, "You are free to go, run before I change my mind." The man leapt to his feet and took off running. The Hyena man turned back to me and said, "I have done as you asked, now I want your body!" I smiled up at him, baring my fangs and said, "Come and get me, big boy!" "What manner of creature are you woman? I have never seen a human with such fangs!" "I am a creature of the night, I am vampire!" "I have heard of such creatures. You live off the blood of the living." I replied, "Yes, but only the most evil of the living, which includes you!" I leapt up, knocking him to the ground. We began the battle dance. He was very strong and I was having trouble handling him. Suddenly he had me pinned to the ground. I could feel his manhood growing against my leg. I thought, "Oh god, he is going to rape me!" He smiled at me with his sharp teeth showing and said, "You are mine!" I screamed, but before he could take me he was lifted into the air. Camaz had the beast high above his head. He brought the Hyena Man down onto his knee, breaking the beast's back. He threw the body into the woods, and ran up to me asking, "Are you alright, my dear? Did he hurt you?" "No, I am fine. I knew this was the only way we could catch him off guard." We checked the area for more of his kind, but we could not scent any others. So we headed back to our plane. On the way, we hunted as I was very thirsty.

CHAPTER 7

A TIME OF PEACE

It had been three years since our last battle with the hunters. Everything had been very quite and peaceful. Our children were all happy with their families. We were one big, happy family! Camaz told me, every night, how much he loved me and made love to me as if it was our first time. We had been to our island many times and had enjoyed walking in the sun together. Jade had returned home after completing college and had settled in nicely. She was so beautiful. I saw both her father and me in her features. Her stunning, emerald green eyes would steal any man's heart alive or undead. One night while I was in the study reading she entered the room and said, "Good evening, mother. I have something I would like to discuss with you if it is alright." I smiled at her, closed my book and said, "Of course my dear, you know you can come to me anytime you need." "I have been thinking, I would like to have a

party so I can see all of my old friends from school." I smiled and said, "I don't see a problem with that. Let us go speak to your father." We headed to the courtyard. Camaz was there with Dempie Jr. They were practicing with their swords. I watched as Camaz moved with speed and grace. My god, the man makes my heart sing! I called to him, "My dear, can you spare us a few minutes? We need to speak with you." He turned, raising his sword to us and said, "Anything for my beautiful ladies!" He told Dempie they would resume later. He walked to us asking, "What do my ladies wish of me?" We proceeded to tell him of Jade wanting to have a party and invite all of her friends. He answered, "Anything for my beautiful daughter. Shall your mother and I begin the party plans?" "Yes father, that would be wonderful! I will get a list for the invitations together and give it to mother." He smiled and said, "As you wish." He grabbed my hand, pulling me with him. "Come, my queen, I am very hungry. Let us hunt!" So off into the beautiful summer night we ran. We arrived in town a few minutes later leaping to the top of a building. I closed my eyes and let my sense of smell range out. Soon I picked up on a delicious smell. I opened my eyes and smiled saying, "There, that house. Our dinner awaits, my love." We leapt from the building, landing on the street. We began creeping towards the house. I stopped and tested the air around the house. I counted a total of three, two men and a woman. They were all evil. I also smelled for innocents, but couldn't locate any. I smiled at Camaz and said, "Dinner is served!" He smiled and went around to the back of the house. He knew the game oh so very well. I went up to the door and knocked. Soon the woman came to the door and asked, "Can I help you?" I explained my car had broken down a few blocks away and asked if I could use the phone to call a tow. She invited me in. The two men were in the living room watching TV. The woman led me into the kitchen where the phone was located. I picked it up and pretended to dial. I asked her the address. She gave it to me. I pretended to tell the tow company the address to pick me up at. I hung up the phone and said, "The man said they would be here in about an hour. Is it alright if I wait here?" "Sure, would you like something to drink?" "That would be nice, thank you." She went to the fridge and returned with a can of soda, handing it to me. I thanked her. We went back into the living room. She told the others that I was going to wait there for the tow truck. Those people were so evil that my throat was ablaze with desire! I didn't know how much longer I could play the game. I heard Camaz, in my head, saying, "Shall we, my dear? I am so very hungry!" I replied, "Yes, so am I. Come on down." About a minute later he entered the room. The men jumped up from their seats. One of them said, "How in the hell did you get in here?" Camaz smiled at the man and said, "Why, through the open window." The man saw Camaz' fangs. I could smell the fear rolling off of him. I stood up, put the soda down and said, "Well guys, the party is over. We are very thirsty!" I leapt on the woman, knocking her to the ground. She fought me, trying to get me off of her. It caused her heart to race, pumping the blood faster. It ignited my killing instincts. I pushed her head to the side and stuck. I sank my fangs deep into her throat. I looked over to Camaz. He had already drained one man and was after the other. I continued to drink, enjoying every drop of her sweetly evil blood. Once I had finished, I stood up and wiped the blood from my mouth. Camaz rose from his second victim and came to me asking, "Are you full, my queen?" I said, "Yes, she was quite yummy!" He laughed saying, "Then let us go home!" We left the house and took to the sky, heading home. We arrived a few minutes later, said our good nights and retired to our quarters. When inside I asked, "I am going to take a hot bath, would you like to join me, my love?" He gave me a big smile and said, "I would love to!" While I was running our bath, we discuss Jade's party. I told Camaz that along with her friends we were going to invite all eligible males in our lands and from afar. He said, "My dear, we do not have to do that. She has the choice of who she wants to be with. Maybe it will be one of her friends from school." We got into the bath. I laid my head back onto his chest. He began to wash me. Oh, how I loved when he washed my body! I felt him kiss my shoulder and heard him whisper, "You have the body of a goddess. I love every inch of you!" I raised my head to kiss him. He picked me up, turning me to face him. I stared into his glorious green eyes and said, "Oh, how you make my heart sing! I love you so much!" He pulled me back to his lips and kissed me passionately. He ignited the fire between my legs. I moaned and said, "My need is great, my love. I need you now!" He put his hands around my waist and lifted me to him. I felt as he entered me. I began to scream his name. With slow, steady strokes he caused me to tremble with the coming orgasm. He sensed my urgency and quickened his strokes, pushing me over the edge. I threw my head back screaming, "Yes, my love. That is it! Faster I am almost there!" He stood up in the tub, still buried deep inside me. I began to ride him like a wild stallion. Faster and faster until I exploded. I screamed out his name, locked my legs tightly around him and let the orgasm take me. This ignited his passion to the extreme. He grabbed my buttocks and began to pound faster and faster. Suddenly he bit into my neck. I screamed out in pleasure and bit him. It caused him to explode inside me. He carried me to our bed and fell on me, exhausted. We laid there panting wildly. I smiled at him and said, "My god, you're fantastic! You please me in every way possible!" His whole face lit up, "I am so proud I please you. I would do anything in my power to make you happy, my queen!" He kissed me tenderly. A few minutes later I fell asleep knowing this man was mine for all of eternity. The next evening I got up, dressed and began to plan Jade's party. A few hours later she brought me a list of friends she wanted to invite. I contacted our printers and ordered the invitations. There would be a hundred in all, including her friends, family, our friends and of course all eligible males, royal or otherwise. I told Camaz I wanted to go into town to the dress shop where we first met and pick out my dress for the party. Also, I asked him to make reservations at the restaurant he took me to on our first date. For you see the next night would be our fortieth anniversary since the wonderful night he made all of my dreams come true. A few weeks before I had gone into town to find the perfect anniversary gift for him. I had gone to the weapons shop were I had purchased his matching daggers. I knew how much he loved old swords, so I went through everything they had until I found the perfect sword. The blade was silver with two dragons etched on the base. The hilt was silver as well, with a large blood red ruby on ether side. The shop keeper told me the sword once belonged to a member of the Order of the Dragon. I thought to myself, "This is prefect! Maybe at one time it could have belonged to our good friend Bogdan!" I had him wrap it up and I made a trip to the restaurant to have them store the sword there. Camaz was going to be so surprised. I could hardly wait to see his face! All of the plans had been made for Jade's party and all the invitations had been sent out. The party would be in a week. I had dressed extra sexy for Camaz. We left home and headed into the city, stopping at the dress shop first. I found several gowns I loved, so I modeled them for Camaz one by one. I saved the best for last. It was of emerald green satin, clinging to me in all the right places. It was strapless, showing off my ample breast quite nicely. When I walked out of the dressing room I watched the spark light up his eyes. He smiled saying, "Wow, I must say this is my favorite, All others where nothing more than rags compared to this dress!" "I am so happy you are pleased my husband, for I love it also!" I went back into the dressing room to change. When I came out he had already paid for my dress. We left the shop and headed to the restaurant. I could still remember our first date like it was yesterday. How nervous I was riding to dinner. We arrived and were escorted out back to the very table we sat at all those years ago. The waiter handed us the menus and gave us a few minutes. I stared across the table into his beautiful emerald eyes. "My god, this brings back so many happy memories! I can still remember being caught up in your eyes that night." He smiled at me and said, "Yes and I can still remember when you told me you wanted to spend the rest of eternity in the night with me! That night you stole my heart and I have never looked back. You are my life, my love, my heart!" He stood up reaching for my hand. "Come my queen, let us walk amongst the flowers you so loved." We went to where all of the nightshade was blooming. My god, the smell was intoxicating! I smiled at him and said, "Oh how I remember that night and the wonderful smell of these flowers. I also remember you taking me into your arms, kissing me for the first time. Oh how you made my heart sing and it has been singing every since!" He pulled me to him, kissing me tenderly. He said, "What I remember the best, was when you told me you where not afraid of me and you wanted to spend all of eternity with me!" We kissed again and headed back to our table. The waiter asked if we were ready to order. Naturally, we ordered the same as our first date. I was having so much fun on our date! Of course, we would never eat those meals but we did enjoy the drinks we had ordered. We got rid of most of the food so it looked like we had enjoyed our meal. I signaled for the waiter to bring Camaz's gift. He handed the box to Camaz. I smiled and said, "Happy Anniversary, my darling!" He smiled at me, signaled to the waiter who then handed me a small white box with a red bow on top. I asked, "Shall we open them together?" Camaz smiled saying, "Ready, set, go!" He opened his gift as I opened mine. I stared down at the most beautiful necklace I had ever seen! There were rubies in the shape of the nightshade flowers with a diamond in the center of each delicate flower. "Oh Camaz, it is so beautiful! Thank you, my love!" He looked up from his gift and said, "I had it made special so you will always remember our walk amongst those flowers. My dear this is the best present you have ever given me!" I proceeded to tell him the story of the sword and how it possibly have belonged to his good friend, Bogdan. He told me he was going to call him later to find out. He took the sword from the box, raised it and said, "To my beautiful queen whom I am sworn to protect and even lay down my life. I salute you!" "Oh darling, you make me the happiest woman on this earth! I love you with my whole body, heart and soul!" We rose from our seats and headed out of the restaurant, back to our car. I said, "My love, I am starving! Shall we hunt?" He laughed and said, "Always thinking with your stomach, my queen! Let us return the car to the house then we will hunt." So we drove back home, parked the car and took to the air.

CHAPTER 8

JADE'S PARTY

The night of Jade's party finally arrived. I was in our room getting ready, putting on my dress and brushing my hair. Camaz neared me and said, "My dear, you look stunning tonight. I love that dress on you. It sets my soul on fire!" I smiled at him, "Thank you, my king. Can you latch my necklace please?" I reached into my jewelery box and retrieved the beautiful nightshade necklace he had given me for our anniversary. I handed it to him and he secured it around me neck. He bent, kissing my neck. I reached up, stroking his face and said, "I love you my wonderful husband. You are my heart and always will be!" He helped me up and walked me out to the party. There were many in attendance. A lot of Jade's friends were human, so we had to be very careful. My best friends, Louisa and Marylou, had arrived with their husbands and children. It had been awhile since I had seen them so I went over to the table so we could get caught up on things. Camaz had gone over to talk to

Bogdan and they left for a few minutes. I knew Camaz had taken

Bodgan to see the sword I gave him. Jade came running up to me,

kissed me and said, "Thank you Mother! The party is so

wonderful! Come I would like you to meet some of my very good

friends." She walked me over to a table where two girls and three

boys sat. "Mother, I would like for you to meet my friends Sally,

Melissa, Robert, James and Thomas." "Hello everyone, I am very

pleased to meet you! My daughter has very good friends to come

all the way here to Mexico for her party." The third boy, Thomas

said, "I can see where Jade gets her good looks. You two could

almost pass as sisters!" "Why, thank you, Thomas. You are very

kind." I proceeded to say my goodbyes and headed back to our

table. I sat down and watched the group talking. I noticed Thomas

making small gestures toward Jade. A smile, a wipe of his hand to

remove a lock of hair from her face. I watched as she smiled at

him, but just enough so she didn't show her fangs. I thought to

myself, "Oh my, looks like we might be planning a wedding in the near future." When Camaz returned he reached for me leading me to the dance floor. As we were dancing he told me the sword was indeed one of Bogdan's. He was so happy his eyes sparkled with delight. I proceeded to tell him of the boy, Thomas, and what I had observed. He smiled and said, "So our little princess has found a human to love, as her father had. How wonderful, but has she told him?" "I don't think so. When she smiled at him it was just enough not to expose her fangs." "We will have to see how their relationship goes before we say anything to her my dear. After all, it is her choice whether or not to take a human for a mate as it was mine." As the party progressed late into the night, I watch our daughter dance with her man. I could tell he was very much in love, but I could not tell with Jade. They came to us to say goodnight. They were going out for a moonlight stroll in the gardens. After they left we said our good nights to everyone and went to our quarters to ready for the hunt. I was in the mood to run. So we left through the front entrance so as not to disturb the children in the gardens. I looked into Camaz' eyes, smiled and said, "Tag your it!" I took off running as fast as I could and he was right behind me. We were running like the wind through the woods. Then I stopped dead in my tracks, causing him to run into me. We both tumbled to the ground laughing. He asked, "Why did you do that?" "I don't know, I just felt something. It caused me to stop like someone was calling to me." "But my dear, there is no one for miles." "I know, but I know I heard someone calling my name, how strange." We got up from the ground and took off running again. I did not tell him the voice I heard was male and was calling me 'Little Vampire!' I knew the voice, but just couldn't place it. I had been called that by so many vampires I had lost count. But still, there was something about the voice. We reached downtown and leapt to the top of a building. I closed my eyes letting my sense of smell take over. Soon I caught a whiff of something wonderful. I leapt to the ground and began to follow the scent. There was a man standing on the street corner. The smell of evil was rolling off of him. I was so hungry I didn't even play a game. I pounced on him, knocking him to the ground and struck. I enjoyed the sweetness of his blood. Camaz was still on top of the building watching. All of a sudden I smelled vampire. I looked up from my prey and there in front of me was Tomas, the vampire who had made me break my blood bond with Camaz. He said, "Hello there Little Vampire, so good to see you again!" Camaz leapt from the building, landing in front of me in a protective stance. He yelled, "Stay away from my wife or I will rip you to pieces!" Tomas laughed and said, "I have been watching you Little Vampire, since I released you. I have not once seen the madness you claimed to have, so I have returned to take back what is mine! I take back your release, come to me!" With his words I felt the blood bond with Camaz snap. I screamed out, "No, this is not possible! How could you! I will die before I allow you to take me away from my one true love!" I pulled a dagger from my arm and prepared to die. I looked at Camaz, my heart was breaking. I said, "I no longer feel our bond my love, he has broken it. I cannot bear the pain and loneliness of not having you! I am sorry, my love, goodbye, I love you!" I swung my dagger toward my heart but before it struck true Camaz stopped me, yelling, "No! I will not lose you this way, stop!" The blood tears began to flow down my cheeks. I was in misery. I felt so alone! "My love, I cannot go on without you. I will not allow myself to be taken by him! Please let me end this sorrow for my heart is broken!" He took the dagger from my hand and said, "No, I will give up my life before I will let you take yours!" He turned to Tomas saying, "You have taken from me what is mine, it is my right to challenge you to take her back. The fight will be to the death. We will meet at my castle three days from now in the arena. Now leave this place!" Tomas leapt into the air and disappeared. Camaz took me into his arms, leapt into the air, flying us back home. He took me to our quarters. I was still crying, he wiped the tears from my face and said, "I hate to see you suffer so, my love! I will kill him for what he has done to you! Then I will bind you back to me!" "Do it now! Please, I cannot stand this pain and sorrow!" "I am sorry, my dear, but I cannot do it yet. Right now you are his. I cannot take you back until he is dead. He will always have a hold on you because you went to him of your on free will. The only way to break his bond is to kill him." He took me in his arms, hugging me to him saying, "I love you and always will. I will gladly lay down my life for you because you are my one true love and soul mate!" I cried myself to sleep in his arms. Three days later we were in the arena. I could still remember my fight with the bitch Josefina. Now I had to watch as my love fought for me. Tomas was on one side of the arena ready for battle. Camaz came out near where I was sitting. He had the sword I gave him on our anniversary. He raised his sword to me and said, "I fight for my right to take back what is mine. If I have to lay down my life, I will gladly do it for you my queen!" He turned to face Tomas. I knew my love was a mighty warrior who had lived for hundreds of years, but I did not know of Tomas or his fighting skills. I did know if he defeated Camaz, taking his life, I would not be far behind my love. I had my daggers by my side and was prepared to use them. Astor stood up and announced "This fight will be to the death. The victor shall take the Lady Anne as their prize." I watched as they began to circle each other with their swords drawn. My mighty warrior charged first and the battle began. With each swing of Camaz's sword it was matched by Tomas'. I was so frightened, Tomas seamed to be a very skill swordsman. I knew my husband was also very gifted. I watched in amazement as they moved faster and faster until they were just a blur. I could smell both of their blood, so I knew they each had inflicted wounds. I watched as they jumped back away from each other. Camaz had taken a hit to his chest and he was bleeding badly. Tomas had also received just as wicked a wound. I could tell they both were weak from the blood loss. I watched in amazement as Camaz leapt into the air, landing in front of Tomas, knocking his feet out from under him, making him fall to the ground. Camaz raised his sword and delivered the fatal blow. At that moment, I felt the tie to Tomas sever. I still could not feel Camaz and my bond. Camaz wiped the blood from his sword and raised it to me saying, "I have delivered the killing blow. I take back what is mine! You are mine and I am yours!" He sheathed his sword, came to me, picking me up into his arms. He carried me back to our quarters, laid me down on our bed and said, "I take back what is mine!" He struck, sinking his fangs into my neck and began to drain me. Slowly I felt my life being drained away. I had become very weak from the blood loss. Then I felt my heart come alive, beating feverishly in my chest. He stopped drinking, reared back and struck again, but withdrew just as quick. I felt his gene take hold, setting my soul on fire. I felt the fire begin to build within me as his gene began to burn through my veins. But I did not scream in pain asking for death as before, I welcomed it as I felt our bond begin to take hold. The fire was engulfing my heart, trying to rip it from my chest. But I did not fight, I allowed it to incinerate my heart. For I knew when the fire won, I won!

Suddenly I felt my heart give in to the fire, taking it's last beat. I laid there in total bliss and opened my eyes. Camaz was staring down at me with a smile on his face. I felt my dead heart come alive and sing for him. I leapt into his arms, kissing him madly. He broke the kiss saying, "Welcome back, my one true love. I can feel our bond and it is stronger than ever before." I smiled at him and said, "That is because I gave into the fire, letting it devour me, for there can be no other! Now no one can ever rip me from you again!" He pulled me back to his lips and ignited my passion.

CHAPTER 9

A NEW BEGINNING

It had been a year since Camaz won me back. We had been more in love than ever. Jade had met and fell in love with Bodgan's son, John the night of her party. They were wed six months later. They became rulers in his country. Bodgan had came for a visit, taking a much needed vacation. One evening he and Camaz were out in the courtyard practicing their swordsmanship. I loved watching Camaz with the sword. He was so skilled. I yelled down to them, "Are you boys done playing? I am starving!" Camaz looked up at me, smiled and said, "Always thinking with your stomach, my queen!" "Yes, I am so ready for the hunt! I feel like running tonight my love." "Then run we shall!" I leaped from the balcony landing beside of him. I took off running and yelled, "Catch me if you can!" I heard him approaching me so I took off at full speed, laughing the whole time and as usual I misjudged my steps, tumbling to the ground. He stopped in front of me laughing and said, "Still clumsy as ever, my love!" I answered, "Ha, ha, very funny. Come here!" I reached up, grabbed his hand and pulled him down to me. I started kissing him madly. He broke our kiss and said, "I thought you were hungry, my queen." "Oh yeah, right, dinner! Let's go!" He stood up, pulling me to my feet and we took off running again. Soon we reached the edge of town. We leapt onto a building and perched there, letting our sense of smell fan out. Soon I picked up on a wonderful smell. I leapt to the ground with Camaz right behind me. We began to stalk off in the direction of the scent. We came to a alleyway, I could hear the man in there, but also a innocent. It was a little boy of about eight years. The man had planned on raping and killing the child. My blood began to boil! How could this monster do such a thing! But I had a plan. I was going in claiming I was the child's mother. I knew the boy's name was Billy, as I had heard him tell the man. I told Camaz to go around to the other end of the alley and await my signal. I began calling the child's name, as if I were searching for him. I entered the alley and screamed for the man to get away from my son. I told the boy to come to me and the police were on their way. The man released the boy and he ran to me. I picked the child up, leaving the alley. I signaled Camaz the child was safe. About a minute later I heard the man start to scream but it didn't last long. Camaz came out with a smile on his face. We left, heading for the nearest police station and dropped the child off there. Afterward we continued the hunt for my meal. As we stalked the streets I picked up on a scent. I pointed to the east and we took flight. We spotted my target standing on a street corner. I swooped down, picked him up and took to the air again. He was fighting me but it did no good. I soon reached the woods. I dropped down into an open area and said to the man, "For all the evil you have done, I claim your life!" I then struck. His deliciously sweet blood set my soul on fire. I drank him down until he was dry. I dropped his lifeless body to the ground. Camaz came up to me and asked,

"Have you had your fill for the night, my love, or shall we hunt some more?" I pulled him to me saying, "No, I have no more need for blood tonight. But I do have need of you, my king!" I pulled him to my lips, kissing him passionately. The next thing I knew we were rolling around on the forest floor, removing our clothes. I laid there naked, all of me for him to see. I smiled up at him. He smiled back and said, "You are so beautiful in the moonlight, my dear! Oh how I crave your beautiful body!" I pulled him back down to my lips showing him just how much I needed him. A few hours later we returned home and prepared for our long sleep. A few days later we said goodbye to our good friend Bogdan, telling him to return for another visit soon. He promised he would in the near future. In a few days we would be going to our island I could hardly wait to walk in the sun again, I had so craved it over the last year. That night we had much more important things to do. We had received word there had been werewolves attacking a town nearby. We dressed in our battle gear. I had put on my full leather body suit. I placed my sword behind my back and fastened my daggers to my arms. I had pulled my hair up into a high ponytail so it would not interfere with me reaching my sword. Once we had dressed we went upstairs to meet with the others. All of the elite squad were there, along with all members of our family. We all headed out into the night heading towards the town where the reports had came from. A few minutes later we were on the outskirts looking down on the town. I sniffed the air looking for the unmistakeable scent of werewolf. Soon I caught it, off toward the other side of town. I signaled everyone I had found the scent. We all took off toward where the werewolves where. We took to the trees so as not to be seen as we approched their encampment. There were at least fifty of the beasts below us. I watched as a large black wolf barked out the commands. It was their leader. He was the one we needed to take out. Once we did, the others would take off like the cowards they were. I signaled to the others we needed to take out the leader. We all drew our swords and leapt to the ground, running toward the werewolf pack. I took the head of the first wolf I came to and continued toward their leader. Suddenly I was knocked to the ground with a beast on top of me. I still had my sword in hand, so I tried to swing, but the beast blocked my blow with his massive paw. He managed to knock the sword from my hand. Suddenly he raked his claws across my face. I screamed out in pain as my flesh ripped. I brought my knees up hard into the beast's chest, knocking the air from his lungs. I slung him off me and jumped to my feet. I ran to where my sword had dropped, but before I could reach it, the beast slammed into my back knocking me to the ground. I felt his claws rip into my back. I screamed out in agony, pulled my daggers from my arms, roll the beast over onto his back and slammed both daggers into his heart. I heard someone yell, "Look out, behind you!" I turned just in time to see the leader charging me. I thought,"Oh shit, got to get out of here!" I leapt straight up into the air. But I had been slowed by the blood loss. He caught my right foot yanking me back down to the ground. I rolled, trying to get away from him and went for my sword. Just as I reached the hilt of my sword he was on me. I was really fighting for my life. The beast was trying to rip my throat out! I slammed my fist into his massive muzzle. I heard the bones break in my hand. But I couldn't stop, I had only stunned him. I reached my sword, swung, catching him across the chest. He screamed out in pain and began to back away from me. I jumped to my feet and charged the beast, but he was to quick and I had lost to much blood. He side-stepped me, causing me to slam into the tree behind him. Suddenly there as blackness! I cried out to our god, "Oh please, please, do not let the darkness take me!" I heard the beast roar. His hot breath was at my neck. I cried out, "Goodbye my one true love." I felt the darkness dragging me deeper and deeper. I laid there in silence. I could not hear anything anymore, not even the battle going on around me. I had to be dead for real. I called out to Camaz over and over in my mind, but I received no response. I heard our god, Cassandra's voice telling me to wake up, that I was not dead, but I would be if I didn't wake up. I came out of the darkness screaming. I opened my eyes just in time to see the beast being ripped to pieces by Camaz. I tried to get up, but I was to weak. He quickly came over, picked me up and said, "It will be alright my love, please hold on for me!" "I am trying my love, but the darkness is all around me trying to claim me as it's own. Please hurry, I don't know how much longer I can hold it off!" He shot straight up into the sky, flying me back to our home. I continued slipping in and out of the darkness. I cried out, "No, please, please do not take we away from my one true love. We have been through so much. I cannot bear the thought of not having his loving arms around me!" I heard him say, "Hold on my love, we are almost there! Fight for me, do not give up!" Hearing his sweet voice with such agony in it sparked something deep within me. I felt the hatred for the darkness begin to build within me. I began to fight with all my might. I would not let the darkness win, taking me away from my love! I could feel his hand on my face, rubbing his healing blood into the wounds. I also felt him pour his blood into the wounds in my back. I began to feel the pull of our bond tugging at my heart. I heard him whisper in my ear, "I have started the healing process, so drink my love. So you can come back to me." I felt him lift me, offering his neck to me. I opened my mouth and bit down. I felt his life giving blood begin to flow into my mouth. Soon my strength began to return. I released his neck, opened my eyes and smiled up at him. He smiled back and said, "Welcome back, my love. I was so worried I had lost you!" I reached up to my face and felt the deep claw marks. I began to cry. He pulled me up into his arms and said, "It will be alright my beautiful queen, they are already beginning to heal. Soon the scars will be completely gone." "But Camaz, I must look hideous, how will I ever be able to captivate my prey!" "There, there, my dear, do not worry yourself. We will not hunt until you have completely healed. We have plenty of stock here for you to feed upon." "Thank you my love, I do not want to see anyone while I am healing, so please explain to our family." After a few minutes he left the room to go get my dinner. While he was gone I rose from the bed and went over to my dressing table staring into the mirror. To my horror, there were four claw marks from the top of my face going across my nose and down to my chin. I began to cry at the sight of myself. How could he even look upon me with my face looking like that! When he returned, seeing me crying, he rushed over to me and asked "What is wrong?" I turned away from him and said, "Oh Camaz, how can you bear to look upon me with my face looking like this!" "Darling, all I see before me is my beautiful queen. I see past the scars and they are of no concern to me!" He pulled me up into his arms, cradling me to his chest and said, "Do not cry, my love, it does not matter to me. You are still as beautiful to me as the first day I laid eyes on you." He pulled my ruined face to him, kissing me tenderly. Two weeks later my face was healing nicely. The scars had become faint pink lines. Soon the would be gone completely. would be able to hunt again. For the time being I was enjoying my meals at home. Camaz had made sure the very finest of evil had been brought to me, because the more evil they were the more powerful the blood was for healing. As I finished my meal he asked, "My love, do you feel up to seeing the children? They are so worried about you and they wish to see you." I looked at myself in the mirror. I could still see the outline of the claw marks, but they were not so bad. "I would love to see our children, send for them." A few minutes later I was surrounded by all of my loving family. Makla and Jade ran up to me, leaping into my arms. I hugged both of them to me. Makla said, "Oh Mother, we have been so worried about you. We are so happy you are well now!" Jade placed her hand to my face and said, "Mother, it is not bad, I promise, soon the scars will be completely gone." So, one by one, all of my children, grandchildren and great grandchildren came to see me. I was so happy to have all of my family around me. Soon some of them would have to leave to go back to their homes so I would spend as much time as I could with all of them. A few days later I was ready to go out hunting. The scars were so faint they were barely visible. I dressed in one of Camaz's favorite hunting outfits, for I knew how much he loved taking it off of me. Due to my severe injuries we had not been able to be together, so I wanted to look my sexiest for him. I came out of the bathroom in my skin tight leather pants and leather bra. I had my spiked thigh high boots on. He smiled at me and said, "My god, woman, you are absolutely ravishing! I could take you right now! You are driving me crazy!" I laughed and said, "Later my love, I feel like running!" So off we ran into the beautiful night I loved so well.

CHAPTER 10

THE HUNTERS RETURN

It had been three years since the werewolf attack. I had completely healed and no longer had the scars on my face. All had been quite during those years and I had been so happy just being with my one true love. Hunting by night and loving by day. He made me so happy. I could scream it to the world. All of the children were doing quite well. Kimsu and Chiyo had been happy together and they had produced many children to populate their world. One evening while we were dressing for dinner I asked, "Camaz, are you still happy with me?" "Why would you ask such a question! I love you with my entire being!" "I don't know, I just feel funny. Like something is going to happen and you are going to leave me!" He rushed over to me, taking me into his arms saying, "Never! Never doubt my love for you. I have loved you from the moment I saw you and that love has only gotten stronger over the years! Nothing will tear you from me ever again!" He kissed me tenderly and said "Now, I do not want to hear of this again. Shall we hunt? I am starving!" I laughed and said, "Hey now, that's my line!" We both laughed and took off into the beautiful summer night. We were running like the wind, side by side. Oh how I loved to run! We stopped for a minute to test the air for prey. We caught a scent and took off running again. We came to the river, leaping over it at the same time and landing on the other side. I could smell our prey, they were close by. I couldn't smell the scent of innocents, so we stalked toward the men. They looked to be smugglers of some kind. By the evil rolling off of them, I would have said they dealt in human trafficking. I said to Camaz, "Let's have some fun with them before we feed!" "As you wish my dear. I know how you love to play the game!" He leapt into the air, going to the other side of where the men were. He landed high up in a tree and waited for my signal. I began to approaching their campsite when all of a sudden I was rushed by two pit bulls. One was jet black, the other, gold and white. They were huge, but as soon as they reached me I looked into their eyes and they sat in front of me. Two men come rushing over, one of them said, "Hey, what did you do to our dogs! I have never seen them do that before." "I don't know, they just ran up to me and sat down." I reached to pet the black one. The other man said, "I wouldn't do that if I were you. He will take your hand off!" I placed my hand at the dog's mouth and he began to lick me. The man said in awe, "Wow, I have never seen him so tame. Are you some kind of witch?" "No, but I have always had a way with animals. They trust me completely." He smiled and asked, "Would you like to join us for dinner?" I laughed to myself and said, "I would love to have dinner with you." We walked into their camp, the dogs were both at my side. The man said, "Amazing." I could smell flesh cooking on the fire, but it had no appeal for me, but their blood did! My blood lust had sprung to life and pulled at me for the attack. I signaled to Camaz in my head "I have grown tired of the game. I am ready to eat." Camaz sprung from the tree, landing in front of the two men and said, "Good evening gentlemen, I see you have met my wife." The startled looks on their faces were priceless. I leapt at the man that brought me into the camp, knocking him to the ground. He looked up at me and asked, "Hey, why did you do that?" I smiled at him baring my fangs and said, "Because I am hungry and you are my meal." I slammed his head to the side and struck. His sweet blood began to flow and I drank him down. Camaz had already drained the other man. I stood up from my prey, wiped my mouth and said, "My, my, how sweet he was. Best meal I have had in weeks!" Just then the two dogs came up to me, sat in front of me and bowed their heads. Camaz announced, "My goodness woman, it seams you have tamed the savage beasts. They have fell in love with you, the way I have. What shall we do with them?" I thought for a minute and answered, "Why, we will take them home with us. They shall be our guardians." "As you wish, my love." I picked up the black and he picked up the gold and white. We leapt into the air carrying them back to our home. Once there he asked, "So, what shall we call our mighty friends?" "I was thinking of names while we were flying home. I will name the black Achilles, after the mighty warrior. The gold and white I will name BamBam, because of his strong heartbeat." So that is how we acquired the newest members of our family and how their names were chosen. They would turn out to be one of our best assets in the future. They were with us during all of our hunting trips. Achilles was mine and BamBam was Camaz's. We had trained them to attack only the wicked and evil of the world, but we had also trained them to fight the hunters. They had learned very quickly and protected us with their lives. While out hunting one evening we caught the scent of hunters. It had been a few years since they have tried to enter our lands. My blood began to boil, how dare they come into our lands. I watched as the hair on the back of Achilles neck rose. He too had scented the hunters and was ready to attack. I rubbed his back, telling him to hold. He sat down on his haunches and waited for my command. Camaz had done the same with BamBam. We began to creep up on the camp. I had counted twenty but there were more coming down the road in cars and trucks. There were too many for us to try and take on by ourselves. So we turned toward home, running as fast as we could. The dogs fell behind, but we couldn't stop to let them catch up. We had to get home to warn everyone. The dogs knew their way home, so I was not worried. We soon arrived back at the castle calling out for everyone. Once they had all gathered, we told them of the hunters and they needed to make ready for an attack. Just then the dogs came running in. They sat beside us, panting wildly. We all quickly left to dress in our battle gear. I knew what those men were capable of, remembering how they took my love from me for 10 years. I would not allow that to ever happen again! With my sword at my back, my daggers in their sleeves and a spare set of daggers in my boots I was ready. I also pulled my crossbow from the weapons cabinet and the arrows I had special made. The arrow tips had a very potent poison on them. The poison would kill an elephant! We rushed out of the room and met up with the others.

We all took off toward the hunters' camp. None of the hunters would leave that place alive! We were right outside of the hunters' camp. There were over fifty of them then. I had a total of twelve arrows, so I leapt up into a tree. At least I would be able to take out that many. Achilles was sitting at the bottom of the tree. He would not leave my side. I reached behind me pulling one of the arrows and loaded it into the crossbow, pulled back and let it fly. The arrow struck my target in the chest and he fell to the ground dead. I reached for my next arrow. But I had been spotted, a hunter was taking aim at me with his own arrow. He let it fly. I leapt to the ground before the arrow could reach me. I loaded my bow, pulled back and fired before he could pull another arrow. My arrow stuck him in the shoulder, but the poison took him. He fell to the ground dead. I had taken out ten of them, but I only had two arrows left. Everyone was in battle with the hunters. I watched as a hunter drew his arrow back, aiming at Camaz. I quickly aimed my crossbow at him, letting the arrow fly. It stuck the hunter in his bow arm, causing him to miss. Then he dropped dead from the poison. I

raised my bow to fire my last arrow when I felt a sharp burning

pain in my arm. It caused me to drop the crossbow. I looked at my

arm, there was an arrow in my bicep. The silver was burning badly.

I yanked the arrow from my arm, screaming while it came out. I

threw the arrow to the ground, reach for my crossbow, pull back the

arrow and let it fly. I took out the man that had wounded me with

his arrow. He dropped to the ground dead. I was out of arrows, so I

dropped the crossbow and drew my sword from behind me. I took

off into the heat of battle. Achilles was right there with me. I

watched as he leapt on one of the hunters, taking him to the ground.

He then proceeded to rip the man's throat out. Immediately he was

by my side again. I smiled at him and said, "My mighty warrior

Achilles!" He barked his pleasure at my words. We went after

another hunter. I swung my sword, but he met it with his own. So

our battle began. He was quite skilled with the sword, but he was

no match for my speed. He swung at me, but missed. I spun around, swung and removed his head. I looked over to where Camaz was in battle with two hunters. I watched in amazement as BamBam leapt onto the back of one of the hunters, sinking his teeth into the man's neck. It had given Camaz the chance he needed, he swung around with his sword and took the second man's head. God how I loved to watch him. He was so fluid in his movements. I watched as he went after another hunter. He leapt, knocking the man to the ground and snapped his neck like a twig. I was not paying attention to my surroundings, all of a sudden I was knocked to the ground by two hunters. One was trying to hold my arms, while the other was over me with a silver spike. But before he could strike, Achilles leapt on him, knocking him away from me. I watched in horror as the man rammed the spike into Achilles's chest. He screamed out in pain. I was quickly to my feet running at the man. I removed one of my daggers and threw it at him, striking him in the heart. He fell to the ground dead. I ran up to Achilles, pulled him into my lap and began to cry for my brave warrior. Camaz came up to me to let me know all of the hunters had been defeated. I looked up at him with tears running down my face and said, "Oh Camaz, my heart is breaking. He has given his life protecting me!" He crouched down and said, "I am sorry for the pain you are feeling right now love. Is he still alive?" "Just barely, the spike has nicked his heart, he is bleeding to death." "My love, he is yours, as you are his. You can save him." "But how, I do not have the power to heal an animal." "No but you can give him our life. Pass the gene to him. But you must do it quickly, for he is dying!" I looked down at my poor Achilles and said, "My brave warrior, I shall give you life for saving mine." I struck, but I recoiled just as quickly, leaving my gene behind. I watched as the fire began to take him. I pulled him up into my arms, shot up into the sky and flew him home as quickly as I could. I knew the burning was going to drive him wild, so I took him down to one of the holding cells, locking the door behind us. I would not leave him until the change was complete. I knew he would not hurt me, so I sat on the cot with him in my lap., talking to him soothingly, letting him know I was there and would not leave his side. He only burned for a little over a day. I heard his strong heart take it's final beat, he looked up at me with the most stunning golden eyes and licked my face. My heart sang out, for I had my mighty Achilles for all of eternity. Soon after his change, I took him out into the beautiful night.

CHAPTER 11

MY MIGHTY ACHILLES

It had been several years since I changed Achilles. He had been a true and loyal companion to me. We hunted together and, like me, he loved to run. Camaz no longer feared leaving me alone, when he had to go out of town on business. For he knew Achilles would guard me with his life. BamBam had gotten up in years so we had deceived to bring him over as well. But because of their bond Camaz would bring him into our life. I had watched him watching Achilles and I could see the want in his eyes. We had deceived we would turn him after the hunt. Camaz would take him to the holding cells and change him. I stalked the streets looking for prey with Achilles right beside me. I knew how much drug dealers loved pit bulls so we used him to bate them. Achilles was very good at the game. I sat atop a building watching as he went up to the house where we had scented the evils. He went to the door, scratched and began to whine. A man came to the door and the look of joy on his face said it all. He had found his next fighter. I leapt to the street and walked up to the house just as he was trying to get Achilles inside. I spoke, "Why hello there. I see you have found my Achilles. May I come inside I want to give you a reward?." The man smiled and said, "Sure, come on in." I looked down at Achilles and watched him curl his lip into a smirk. That dog never ceased to amaze me. We followed the man into the house. I spotted another man on the couch. I smiled at him but did not show my fangs. We wanted to have some fun first. The man told me to have a seat and asked, "Would you like a beer?" "That sounds nice, thank you." So he went into the kitchen. The other man said, "Lady, that is a beautiful animal. How much do you want for him?" I answered, "Sorry, but he is not for sale." Just then the other man returned with beers. He handed one to me. I accepted it and took a quick sip. I had never liked the taste of beer, but I drank it for the sake of the game. Suddenly the man on the couch stood up and said, "Are you sure you don't want to sell the dog?" "No, he is not for sale." "Then we will take him from you. You are never going to leave this house alive!" I began to laugh and said, "Oh, but that is where you are wrong, you two will not leave this house alive!" With that Achilles pounced on one man, knocking him to the ground and proceeded to rip his throat out. The other man began to scream. I smiled at him, baring my fangs and said, "Game over I am hungry!" I leapt on him and stuck. As I began to drink, he was fighting me wildly, making his heart pump quicker and quicker. It set off my blood lust to a frenzy. I began tearing at his throat until it was in shreds. Slowly I began to lap up the blood as it poured from the wounds until there was none left. I rose up from my prey looking for Achilles. He came bounding up and sat down beside of me. I petted his head and said, "My mighty Achilles, that was quite fun. Let us leave this place so we can check on your brother's progress." We both left the house, leaping into the air heading for home. As soon as we reached the castle BamBam came bounding out, leapt, knocking me to the ground and began licking my face.

He then took off with Achilles. They chased each other around the grounds with the joy of being together again. Camaz came out, took me into his arms and said, "Oh, my queen, I am so happy! I have you for all of eternity and now we have our beloved dogs as well!" I said, "Yes my love and look at them, they are so happy!" He pulled me to his lips and said, "Not as happy as I am, I love you!" He kissed me tenderly. We went into our quarters, shutting the door behind us. We knew the dogs would be gone for hours. So it was play time for us. He came up to me and began to undress me. I loved when he took my clothes off, he did it so passionately. He had me striped naked in no time. I began to remove his clothes, for I knew he loved it as well. I dropped to my knees and began to slowly unzip his pants pulling them down over his hips. I took him into my mouth, gently running my fangs down the length of him. This caused him to moan out. He pulled me to my feet and kissed me passionately. He reached behind me grabbing my buttocks and raised me to him. As I felt him enter me, I screamed out in ecstasy.

A few hours later, as we started to fall to sleep when we heard a scratching at the door. Our boys were home. Camaz went over and let them into the room. Achilles came to my side of the bed, laying on the floor. BamBam had done the same on Camaz's side of the bed. We all fell blissfully into our deep sleep. A few weeks later, while we were hunting, I told Camaz I would like to go to the island for a couple weeks. I had been longing to lay in the sun again. He smiled at me and said, "Anything my queen's heart desires, I will provide!" So after our hunt we returned to the castle to let everyone know we were going away for a few weeks. Little did we know that when we returned our empire would be in ruin. But I'm getting ahead of myself. We arrived on the island around 4am. We had brought the dogs with us but had commanded them to stay out of the sun. I could hardly wait until sunrise. He knew how excited I was so we did not sleep. We would have plenty of time later for that. We were sitting on the beach waiting for the sun to rise. I could see the first glimmers of light just over the horizon.

It was so beautiful! I began to feel the warmth on my body. I laid back to enjoy the first rays on my body. I could feel the tingling began, letting me know the change was near. I looked at Camaz and smiled. He was glowing a pale red. I was still amazed at how beautiful he looked in the sun! He smiled back at me and said, "My god, woman, you are stunning in the sunlight!" "As you are, my king!" I rolled to my side, he took me in his arms, kissing me. He pulled me on top of him, lowering me onto his manhood. I screamed out as he entered me, throwing my head back. He started a slow, steady rhythm. I began to rock back and forth. Suddenly he ignited a fire deep within me. The orgasm wracked my body. I screamed out his name, look down at him and he gasped. He told me my eyes had turned crimson red. I smiled at him and said, "I am yours and you are mine. You have ignited the fire in my soul!" He pulled me to his lips, kissing me madly. He flipped me over onto my back and began to thrust faster and faster. I looked up at him, his eyes had also turned crimson red. This sent me over the edge into the abyss. I screamed over and over as he rode me into the sand. We then bit each other at the same time. I felt his sweet blood began to flow into my mouth. I was in complete and total ecstasy. The orgasms roll through my body over and over. I dug my nails into his back causing him to explode. God, if my heart could still beat, it would have exploded! He collapsed on top of me and we laid there in each others arms, panting wildly. Once he caught his breath he asked, "What the hell happen to us?! I have never felt such passion within me! I feel like you have set my soul on fire!" I smiled up at him and said, "My love, I think that is exactly what happened to both of us. I watched as your beautiful emerald green eyes turn crimson red as did mine! You set my soul on fire, igniting a passion deep within me!" He smiled and said, "Woman, you are amazing. You are always surprising me. You bring out the very best in me!" My god, the man made my heart sing! We laid on the sand, letting the sun's warmth engulf us. About an hour later we returned to the house to make ready to hunt. The dogs were so happy to see us. Achilles ran up to me, knocking me to the floor and began to lick me profusely. I laughed, telling him to stop, but all the while I wanted him to continue. Oh, how I love that dog! We had been on the island for two weeks and it was time to go home. I would miss being able to walk in the sun, but I missed my family and friends also. We loaded up the speedboat and head back home. About an hour later we arrived. Immediately I felt something was wrong. The feeling of dread over took me! He looked at me and saw the pain in my face and asked, "What is wrong?!" "I don't know, but we need to get below, something is very wrong!" We raced into the cave with our swords drawn. The dogs were right beside us. We entered the cavern and there were dead all around us! We ran to the first body, it was Dempie Jr. I screamed, "Oh god, what has happened here? Hurry, my love, we must find the children!" We raced into the castle and there were many dead in there as well. All of our elite squad had been massacred. We rushed into the throne room and there on the floor dead were both of our sons! I screamed in agony, "No, no, please, not my children!" I ran to Mikel, looking into his lifeless eyes and the same with Camazotz. They both had silver arrows embedded in their chests. I heard my beloved cry out in pain. I ran to him and there I found our daughter Makla dead also. I dropped to my knees and began to cry. I looked at Camaz with the blood tears running down my face and said, "Camaz where is Jade? Have you seen her?" "No, my love, I have not. Let us go quickly, as I have not seen any of the other woman either. I hope they are safe in the hiding place below." We reached below quickly and there was dead down there also. I began to run like the wind toward the hiding place we had constructed so many years ago. When we arrived, the entrance was wide open. I screamed in horror, "Oh, god, no! They have gotten in here also!" We ran into the room and there on the floor dead was Iris, Kim and all of the other women. We began to search for Jade but she was no where to be found. We searched the entire castle and the grounds for her, but she was not there.

Suddenly I heard a howl, it was Kimsu. We quickly ran toward the sound. We found him and his mate mortally wounded. I dropped to my knees and said, "Oh, Kimsu, I am so sorry! What happened here?" In a pained voice he said, "My lady, we were attacked by thousands of hunters. Everyone fought bravely but there was just to many of them!" I asked, "Kimsu, have you seen Jade? We cannot find her anywhere!" "She was taken by the hunters. We tried to stop them but they took us down." I heard his mate cry out. I looked to her, she was dead. I turned back to Kimsu and watched as the life left his eyes. I could feel the hatred began to build within me, stoking the fire in my heart! I looked at Camaz with my eyes ablaze and said, "We will hunt down every hunter on this planet until we have eradicated the whole lot! I will not rest until we find our daughter alive or dead. But I promise they will all pay for taking the lives of our children, family and friends!" So all that night we buried our dead. There was so many it took us until daybreak. But I did not care. I stood in the sun and for the first time

I did not enjoy it. The hatred was consuming me to my core. We went to sleep until sundown. When we arose, the hunt for the vampire hunters began. We dressed in all of our battle gear, I made sure I brought plenty of arrows for my crossbow. With everyone dead, we became King and Queen again. We had sworn on our children graves we would not rest until all vampire hunters, all over the world, were dead. We took off into the night, with our dogs beside us, and began the search of our lands for the hunters. We scented the air for our prey and soon picked up on them. We followed the scent until we reached a large encampment. We leapt into the trees so not to be seen. I began to search for our daughter's scent. But she was not there. I pulled my crossbow around and loaded the first arrow. I smiled at Camaz and said, "Now they shall pay!" I let the arrow fly striking the first man I spotted, hitting him in the chest. He fell to the ground dead. I pulled another arrow, loaded and let it fly. I continued until I had taken all out with the exception of two. We lept from the trees, knocking the two men to the ground. I straddled my victim with a arrow poised above his heart and said, "Where is my daughter, hunter?" He looked up at me smiling and said, "You will never find her. She has been taken far away from here. Go ahead and kill me, I do not care!" I looked him in the eye, catching him with my stare. I said, "Now, you are going to tell me where my daughter is!" He was fighting my mind control, he was very strong willed. But I watched as he began to give in to my request. He then spoke, "All I can tell you is she was taken somewhere in the United States. We were not told the location for just this reason." I raised the arrow and drove it straight through his heart. He died instantly. Camaz took the head of the other man with his sword. I stood up, spitting on the man's body. The hatred was burning all the way to my soul. I turned to Camaz saying, "We will travel to America first in search of our daughter. Let us go back to the castle to make ready for the trip. I am starving, but it will have to wait until we get to the states." We did not have much night left so we needed to get to the plane before sunrise. Our pilot had been alerted and had the plane ready for the trip. We would be starting in Washington and working our way across the country. We reached the plane and boarded. Camaz went to the pilot letting him know after we landed in Washington we would have no need of him until we returned to Mexico. We arrived in Seattle around 9pm, left the plane, unload all of our battle gear and left on foot, the dogs followed close behind. Our first stop was at the home of the king and queen, the ones we rescued so many years ago. We were greeted by their top adviser, Nicholas. He was the one that took Astor's place when he joined us. Nicholas told us they were attacked and many had died there as well, including the king and queen. He also told us the attacks had been taking place all over the country. All surviving vampires had gone underground. We told him how our entire family was slaughtered back home. We told him our youngest had been taken captive and brought to the states. He told us he would take us to where all of the vampires had gone underground. They were located in a remote mountain in North Carolina. He contacted his pilot to have his plane made ready for the trip. We loaded all of our gear and everything Nicholas had into his van and headed for the airport. We took off and the trip lasted about four hours. It was midday, so we retired to the belly of the plane to await sunset. Nicholas had called his friends in North Carolina and they would be picking us up. While waiting I had paced back and forth. The anger was still building in me, but also a glimmer of hope our daughter was still alive somewhere. Camaz came to me, taking my in his arms, trying to comfort me. "I know how angry you are, my love, as I am, but we will not rest until we find Jade, I promise!" I look at him with tears in my eyes and said, "I just hope we find her alive. I could not bear to lose all of our children! My heart still aches for all that has been lost! She is all we have left now. I can no longer give you children my love, this so saddens my heart!" He said, "I feel your pain, my queen, but even if we have lost Jade, you still have made me the happiest man on earth with all you have given me!" He raised my chin and kissed me tenderly. It was sunset when we disembarked the plane and headed into the mountains. When we reached as far as we could go by car, we took to the air, flying toward the highest mountain top. We landed at the entrance of a cave and began our decent down to where the other vampires, who had survived the hunters attacks, where located. We went down miles deep into the mountain until we reached a huge cavern. There were many vampires there. We were told the kings and queens of the North and West were there. We went to meet with them. We proceeded to tell everyone what had happened in our country and about our daughter. The king of New York told us they had received intel of a young female vampire that was captured in Mexico and she was being held in Florida somewhere. I just knew it was Jade. I said to Camaz, "Oh baby, I just know it is her! We must leave for Florida immediately!" I turned and said to the king, "Did they say where she is being held?" "All we know is she is being held somewhere in central Florida. The hunters' main compound is located there." I said to the king, "We must go to find our daughter. But I promise when we return, we will help you eradicate all hunters from your lands!" The following evening we prepared for our trip to Florida. It had been three days since we had hunted and I had become very thirsty. We went to the holding cells to feed as we did not have time for the hunt. Once finished we left, flying back down to the foot of the mountain where a car had been left for us. We loaded all of our gear in the trunk and backseat then left. It was a twelve hour drive to Florida so we pulled over just before daybreak to find a cemetery to sleep. The follow evening at dusk we rose to make the final two hour drive. That gave us plenty of time to search for the compound. We arrived in Orlando and started our search from there. As Camaz drove, I scented the air for hunters and our daughter. Soon I picked up on the hunters' scent. There were many, so I knew we were going in the right direction. But I still had not picked up our daughter's scent. But even if she was not there, none of them were going to live! The scent became very strong, close to a very large preserve. It sat right in between Orlando and Tampa. It was called Tenoroc preserve. We left the car and got all of our battle gear on. We took off into the woods in search of the hunters' compound. We let the dogs lead the way as their sense of smell was even keener than ours. We were deep in the woods. The dogs had alerted us they had found the camp. We took off running, the whole while I was testing the air for Jade's scent. But still nothing. I thought to myself, "If I find out they have killed her every last one of them will pray for death before I am finished with them. They do not call me Death's Deliverer for nothing." We had discovered the hunters' camp was underground in an old phosphate mine. There were five guards at the entrance. I quickly took them out with my crossbow. We went below. I could smell many hunters down there. I suddenly picked up a faint whiff of our daughter. I said to Camaz, "That way, I have caught her scent!" We quickly headed toward where I had scented her. We had to be vary careful so we were not spotted by the hunters. We had to take them by surprise. We reached the area where Jade's scent was the strongest. The room was guarded by five men with weapons that could take us out. So we had be very careful. I knew I could take two out with the crossbow. We would send the dogs after the others. The hunters had no idea the dogs were vampires. Camaz would go for the last man. I made a circling motion with my hand for the dogs to go around. They took off on my command. When they were in place I drew two arrows from my back, placing one in my mouth for easy access and placed the other in my bow, letting it fly. As soon as I did, I grabbed the other from my mouth and loaded, letting it fly. I took out both of my targets. Suddenly the dogs were on their two targets. The fifth man was so stunned he didn't see Camaz coming. I watched as my beloved removed the man's head. I ran to the door, ripping it from it's hinges. I rushed inside and cried out, "Jade, where are you!" I heard a moan coming from another room. I ran into the room and there was our daughter strapped down to a table. She had a silver dagger in her chest. I ran over to her screaming out, "No! This cannot be! I will not lose the

only child I have left!" The tears began to flow down my face. She

smiled at me and said, "It is alright, Mother, you have given me the

happiest years of my life. I am not afraid to die." Camaz was on the

other side of her holding her hand. She smiled at him and said, "Do

not be sad for my loss, Father, you and mother must go on to

protect the vampire world from this plague!" I looked to my

husband and said, "Please, please, there must be something we can

do. I cannot bear to lose another child! Camaz, please do

something!" He looked at the dagger in her chest and said, "I am

sorry, my dear, but there is nothing I can do. The dagger is to close

to her heart to remove." I screamed out in agony, my heart was

being ripped from my chest. Jade said, "Please do not cry, Mother.

I cannot stand to see you in so much pain. Just know I love both

you and Father. I will be with you both, even in death." Then she

took her final breath. I dropped onto her lifeless body and wept.

Camaz reached for me, pulling me to his chest and said, "She is and my heart is breaking, as is yours, my queen. We must be strong for her. We must avenge her death!" I looked at him and watched as the blood tears flowed down his face. I could see the pain and anguish in his beautiful eyes. My heart broke into a million pieces. We had lost all of our children and every hunter on Earth better prepare themselves, for Death's Deliverer was coming!

CHAPTER 12

THE BEAST WITHIN ME

It had been one year since we lost all of our family and friends to the hunters. We swore on our daughter's death bed we would avenge her death. Even if it took us all of eternity. The memory of all of our children's dead bodies were burned into our memories forever. I still awoke screaming every night for them. The nightmares were never ending. It had caused me to grow cold and vicious over time. We had gone back to our country and were ridding our beloved Mexico of the vermin. Once we finished there we would go all over the world. We would not rest until we had eradicated every last vampire hunter! We were stalking the dark silent streets in search of the vampire hunters. The hatred was so strong in me. It was as if a great beast had risen from within me. I hungered for their deaths! Camaz was right beside me as we stalked for our prey. Achilles and BamBam were in front of us scenting the prey. Suddenly they stopped in their tracks, sniffed the air and alert us they had found hunters. We took off running toward the scent. Soon we came upon an encampment with many hunters. I signaled for the dogs to go around to the other side. Camaz and I leapt into a tree high above the hunters. The anger was building within me, I began to see red. I pulled my crossbow up and loaded an arrow. I placed two more in my mouth. There were three guards at the entrance to the encampment. I let the first arrow go, it struck one man in the chest and he went down. I pulled another from my mouth, loaded it and let it fly, striking the second man. I readied to fire the third but the man had alerted the others in the compound. About 15 to 20 men came running out to where we were. I only had nine arrows left, so I began to fire at them as they come out. I heard one of the men yell, "Watch out! That is Death's Deliverer with the bow, she is deadly accurate with that thing!" I took him out just as he spoke my name. I had let all of my arrows fly, so I dropped the crossbow to the ground, pulled my sword from my back and leapt down and ran toward the other men. I could see the fear in their eyes. I thought to myself, "Good, you need to fear me!" I leapt at one of the men, taking his head as I landed. I took off running after the others. Camaz had three of them backed up and was moving so fast they couldn't see his sword coming. He removed all their heads. I watched as my mighty Achilles and BamBam went after four of them. I watched as they leapt, taking down two of the men. Both of them rip the men's throats out at the same time. As always, I was not paying attention to what was going on around me. I suddenly felt something strike me in my neck. I dropped to the ground screaming. I reached up and felt the dagger deep within my neck. The next thing I knew I watched as Achilles ran to me and took a protective stance in front of me. The man that had thrown the dagger was charging towards me with his sword drawn. I watched as Achilles leapt at the man like a sleek black panther, knocking him to the ground and proceeded to rip his throat out. He came back to me, taking a protective stance again. By then the silver in the blade was burning my throat badly. But I had to get up, there were still more of them to kill. I reached up, pulling the dagger from my neck, screaming the whole time. The blood began to pour from the wound. I screamed for Camaz as the darkness was coming for me. He quickly ran over to me, bit his wrist and let the blood pour into the wound. I felt it begin to seal. But I was too weak from the blood loss to get up. I saw a hunter pulling back his bow and let the arrow fly. I screamed to Camaz to look out but it was too late. The arrow struck him in the chest and he went down. I began to crawl over to him. I told Achilles and BamBam to go after the man that had fired the arrow, as he was the only one left. They took off like the wind, knocking the man to the ground. I heard him scream once, then silence. By then I had reached my beloved. I looked at the arrow in his chest. Luckily it had struck him on the right side, missing his heart. I told him I was going to remove the arrow and to brace himself. I reached for the shaft of the arrow and pulled it out as quickly as I could. He screamed in agony. I bit into my wrist and let my healing blood flow into his wound. I watched as the wound began to seal. We were both very weak from the blood loss and needed to feed. I called for the dogs, they came running and sat down beside us. I told them they need to go find us food and bring it back. Camaz pulled me to him and said, "I am sorry I did not protect you, my queen! I promised you I would not let anything happen to you, but I have failed you!" I told him to stop talking like that, he had been in a heated battle and could not help without getting himself killed. He smiled at me and said, "My dear, you have a true and good heart, that is why I love you so much!" Then we heard the dogs returning. They were dragging our food by their necks, but had not bit down. Achilles brought a man to me and BamBam took his to Camaz. We both struck and began to drink. The man's sweet evil blood began to run down my throat. I could feel my strength returning with each drop of his blood. When I had drained him I looked to Camaz. His color looked much better. He rose from where he was, reached for me, pulling me into his arms. He leapt into the sky, flying me back home. We arrived back at the castle, the silence was deafening. I so missed the sound of our family and friends! Camaz took me below to our quarters, laid me on the bed and offered me his neck saying, "Drink, my beautiful queen, and get well for me." I bit down gently and began to drink. His life giving blood began to energize me. I released my hold on his neck and turned mine to him. He bit and began to drink. I felt every nerve ending in my body spring to life. I grunted out my passion. He released his hold on my neck, looked down at me and said, "Are you trying to tell me something, my dear?" I pulled him to my lips, showing him just exactly what I was trying to tell him. The next thing I knew he had entered me. I screamed out his name as he thrust deeply. His blood had set my soul ablaze with passion! As he began a slow steady stroke, he brought me over and over. I felt the shivers of pleasure run down my back. I knew he was close, so I bit him. As I drank, I brought him to a shattering climax. We laid there panting wildly in each others arms. I rolled over onto my side, looked into his beautiful eyes and said, "You are amazing, my love! I have never felt such passion, you set my soul on fire!" He pulled me to him, kissing me tenderly. About an hour later we fell asleep in each others arms. That night I dreamed of our god, Cassandra. In the dream she told me all of children were there with her and happy. She told me there were still many hunters and we needed to go after all of them. The anger and pain in her voice pulled at my heart. I felt her loss of all of her children through out the world. I made her a promise I would destroy all vampire hunters or die trying! I heard her sweet voice telling me she believed in me and she knew I was her champion. I awoke from the dream. I told Camaz of the dream and what our god had said about our children. I also told him we were her champions and it was our job to destroy all of the vampire hunters all over the world. We got up, dressed in our battle gear and headed out into the night. I stared up at the beautiful night sky and for the first time since our loss I felt my heart soar at the sight. Oh how I loved the night sky! But my heart was still hard. I said to him, "Let us go, we need to destroy as many as we can before the sun comes up." We took off running through the forest, the whole time we were scenting the air for hunters. But first we had to feed. I caught a wonderfully evil smell off to the south. I smiled at him and we took off in the direction the smell was coming from. We soon came upon two men sitting at a campfire, the smell of evil was rolling off of them, setting my throat ablaze. Normally I would have played the game, but I did not crave the game anymore. All I could think about was destroying as many hunters as I could get my hands on. I leapt at one of the men, Camaz leapt at the other. We both struck at the same time, draining our victims dry. We leapt into the night sky and began to hunt for the hunters. Soon we picked up on a scent off to the west. We followed the smell all the way into town. We sat down atop a building. I closed my eyes and let my sense of smell take over. Down the street there was a large house brightly lit. We leaped from the building, landing on the street below. We stalked up the Down the street there was a large house brightly lit. We leapt from the building, landing on the street below. We stalked up the street to where the house was. We took a quick look through an open window. There were five men and two women in the living room. We went around to the back of the house. There were three more in the kitchen. We could also hear four more upstairs. So there was fourteen in all. I had a full set of arrows, enough to take out twelve of them. I told Camaz I was going upstairs to take out those four first. I told him to wait for my return and we would go after the others. I leapt to the second floor and entered through an open window. I began creeping down the hallway. I stop dead in my tracks and listen closely. I could hear two in one bedroom, the other two in another. I approached the first door and kicked it open. I fired my crossbow at the woman in the bed, my arrow struck her in the chest. I had another arrow in my mouth. I quickly loaded it into the bow and let it fly, taking out the man in the bed. I left the room heading for the other two in the other room. I took them out quickly and leaped from the window landing next to Camaz. We quickly made our plan for taking the others. I was not dressed to play the part of an innocent, so we had deceived on a different approach. We both went around to the back of the house where the kitchen was located. We called Achilles and BamBam. They came bounding up to us and sat at our feet. I stooped down and whispered in Achilles's ear for him and BamBam to go up to the door and scratch like they were wanting in. I watched as they both ran up onto the porch and begin scratching on the door. A few minutes later a woman came out of the house and called to the others to come see the beautiful Pit Bulls she had found. The other three men came out from the kitchen. I watched as my boys went to work, setting the hunters at ease, as if they were harmless. I smiled to myself for I knew better. I released an arrow and took out the woman on the porch. I watched as the men ran to her. I whistled to Achilles to start the attack. He knocked one of the men down. BamBam took another man down. They proceed to rip the men throats out. There was only one man left, Camaz ran for him, knocked him to the ground and broke his neck. Afterward we went around to the front of the house. We only had seven left in the living room. They didn't call me Death's Deliverer for nothing. I walked right up onto the porch, knocked on the door and waited to be invited in. A man came to the door, opened it and eyed me up and down. I could see the lust in his eyes. Boy was he in for a surprise! He invited me into the house. I surveyed the living room, noting where everyone was located. I relayed the information to Camaz. The other four men in the living room began to look at me with lust in their eyes. I was going to play with them. I said to the man who had invited me in, "Your not going to let your friends look at me like that are you?" He turned and said, "What are you talking about?" "Well, I thought we had made a connection back there, I guess I was wrong, forgive me." I batted my eye lashes at him. I could almost hear the wheels begin to turn in his puny brain. He told the others we were going outside to talk. We left the house and went onto the porch. He pulled me to him and tried to kiss me. I pulled away from him telling him to stop. I was not interested in him. The next thing I knew he smacked me in the face and said, "I should have known, you are nothing more than a cock tease!" I heard my beloved's voice, "How dare you strike my wife! I will tear you to peaces right here hunter!" I watched as the fear began to build in the man. He knew what we were. He started to scream but before it could escape his lips I had him down on the porch with my hand over his mouth. I then snapped his neck. I stood up from the man and said, "I have tired of this game! Shall we take care of the others?" Camaz smiled at me and said, "Your wish is my command, my queen!" I called the dogs to us and we made ready to finish the rest of the vermin inside. Camaz kicked the door in and the dogs ran in first. I watch as they took down two and went after two more. I pulled my sword from my back and made ready for battle. The only woman left rushed me. She also had a sword. We begin to fight. She was a very skilled swords woman, but she was no match for me. I sidestepped her attack and came back around, catching her in the arm. She screamed out in pain and charged me again and swung. I dropped to the ground and came up, knocking her feet out from under her and she went down. I swung my sword downward, taking her head. I looked to where Camaz was just in time to see him take out the last man. I ran over to him and asked, "Are they all dead?" "Yes, my love. I do not scent any others here." We left the house and headed back to the castle.

CHAPTER 13

A NEW FRIEND

It had been two years since we had cleared our country of all hunters. We were getting ready to make the trip to America to rid them of all hunters. We had contacted our new friends in the North Carolina Compound and they were awaiting our arrival. We were loading all of our battle gear in to the plane and we went hunting before we left. An hour later we were stalking the dark streets in search of our prey with the dogs right by our side. I watched as the dogs picked up a scent and headed off in it's direction. We arrived at a house a few minutes later. The smell of evil was all around . I had picked up three inside, but I had also scented a vampire! Camaz said to me, "There is a vampire inside. I am not familiar with this vampire so be very careful, my dear!" I reached behind me and retrieved my sword. He did the same. From the scent the vampire in question was upstairs in one of the bedrooms. I had also scented a innocent in the house.

She was upstairs where the vampire was. We watched as he leapt from a window with the woman in his arms. He took her away from the house and then he was back. He spotted us and went into a protective stance. Camaz held up his hand and spoke, "We mean you no harm, we are just here for the hunt." The vampire stood up, coming over to where we were standing. I was behind Camaz just in case the vampire tired something. The vampire spoke, "My name is Vincent, may I ask who you are?" "I am your King Camaz and this is my Queen Anne." He bowed and said, "Forgive me Sires, I did not know it was you. I will leave the evils for you." "You do not have to leave, there is plenty to go around!" After we finished off our dinner we invited Vincent back to the castle. Along the way we told him how we had lost everything and we had vowed to eradicate all hunters from the world. We told him we had finish in Mexioc and would be heading to America in a few hours. He said, "I would like to go with you if possible, sires. I to have lost all of my family to the vermin!" We told him he could accompany us if he wished. Soon after we were on the plane heading to the United States. We had retired to our sleeping quarters and would sleep until we arrived in North Carolina. I had just undressed and I was brushing my hair. Camaz came up to me, taking the brush from my hand and began to brush my hair. I loved it so when he did that! I felt him kiss my neck ever so gently. I stood up and turned to face him. He said, "Do you know how much I love you, my beautiful queen?" I smiled up at him and said, "I'm not sure, would you like to show me?" He pulled me to his lips, kissing me passionately. He picked me up, caring me to the bed. He laid me down, staring me he said, "Your body would put any woman to shame, alive or dead!" I could see the lust building in his beautiful green eyes. I smiled at him and said, "As your body would put any man to shame, my love!" He began kissing my neck. I moaned with the pleasure he was giving me. He kissed down my neck until he reached my left breast and began to suck. I felt his fangs rub up against my nipple, setting my soul ablaze. I grunted out my pleasure and pulled him back to my lips kissing him wildly. I said, "My love, you have set my soul ablaze with need! I need you now!" Suddenly I felt him enter me. I screamed out my pleasure with each thrust. I could feel my climax coming so I yelled, "Faster, my love, I am at the cliff, send me over into the abyss!" He sped up. I felt my climax began to take me. I screamed out his name and raked my nails down his back. He screamed out his pleasure and said, "Anne, you are my heart. Oh how you make me soar with pleasure!" I felt him explode inside of me as I reached my full climax at the same time. He laid there panting wildly. He rose up looking down at me. I could see his total and unconditional love for me in those eyes. I smiled at him and said, "My king, you please me in all ways possible. I will love you until the end of time!" He smiled at me and said "As I will love you, my beautiful queen!" He rolled off of me and pulled me into his arms. I fell to sleep with a smile on my face. That night I dreamed of our children. I saw their births, watched as they grew up into strong young men and women. Watched them fall in love, take mates for life, and all of the beautiful grandchildren and great grandchildren they had given us. I cried tears of joy as I watched all of them. Then my tears turned to sorrow as I looked upon all of their faces as they laid dead in front of me. I cried out in agony. I heard the sweet voice of our god, Cassandra, "I am so sorry you suffer so my child. I can feel you broken heart scream out for all you have lost. But do not despair, there will be more children in your future!" "But how, I was told by the healers I could never have children again after Jade's birth!" "My child, I am god to all vampires. If I say it is so, then it will happen. But first you need to rid our world of all vampire hunters. You are my champion and I have set this task for you and Camaz. There are many good friends awaiting your arrival in North Carolina. They will help you with your quest. Also, I have sent Vincent to help you. He is also one of my chosen champions. He will fight beside of you and is a fierce warrior. I will come to you later in another dream when it is time for you to start having children. So go, my mighty champion and rid our world of this plague!" I awoke from the dream. I felt the plane touch down I quickly told Camaz of my dream and what our god had promised. I had never seen him so happy! We got dressed in our battle gear and departed the plane with Vincent. The dogs were right behind us. Once we were outside of the airport we were met by our friend Jason. He took us to his truck and we loaded up all of our gear and headed off to the mountain compound. We drove up the mountain as far as we could go and took to the air for the final few miles. We reached the entrance to the cave and were greeted by the elite guard and taken below. Once we reached the cavern we went to the war room to find out what had been learned of the hunters. King Michael of the north and King Jasper of the southern nations were awaiting us. They had put a stop to their war for the better of all vampires. For we had to all band together to stop the hunters! We went up to them, said our hellos and listened as they told us all they had found out. As we listened, we were told there were four compounds here. One in Alaska, one in Georgia, one in Ohio and their main compound was in Florida. I said, "I thought we destroyed the compound in Florida!" Jasper answered, "You did, but they have built another in the same spot." I could feel the fire of anger building within me. How dare them rebuild where they slaughtered my daughter! I looked at Camaz and said, "We are going to Florida first!" "As you wish, my queen." A few hours later we were readying to go to Florida. We had loaded up all of our equipment and were now heading for the airport. Once there we loaded all the the equipment onto the plane and boarded. I was so ready to go kill hunters! We had learned the head of the hunters down there was named Jacob and he was the brother of the man I killed. He had sworn he would not stop until all of our kind was destroyed. I would make sure when we got there he would meet the same fate as his brother. I had learned he was the one who plunged the fatal dagger into our daughter's heart! I paced back and forth waiting for our arrival. I was so ready for that battle! Camaz came up to me pulling me into his arms and said, "Do not worry, dear heart, we will take the man, making him pay for taking our daughter's life." I looked at him with tears streaming down my face, her death still fresh in my mind. He wiped the tears from my face and kissed me tenderly. We felt the plane touchdown at the Orlando airport. We quickly dressed in our battle gear and made ready to leave the plane. One of the alliance in Florida was awaiting us with a large van. We loaded up all of our gear and head out to Lakeland. A few hours later we were in the heart of the Tenroc preserve searching for the compound. We knew there should be no other humans there so we tested the air for the blood of innocents. Soon I picked up something. I told them, "There, that way, I can smell many men and women!" I pulled my crossbow around loaded an arrow and made ready for the attack. I had three more arrows clutched between my teeth. I took aim at the first guard, let my arrow fly and loaded the second, taking out another guard. I watched as the third man took off running toward the entrance. I loaded the third, taking him out as well. We all ran down to the entrance of the compound and went underground. I drew my sword from behind me so I could be ready for anything. We came out into the opening of the compound. There were hunters everywhere. We rushed them, catching them by surprise. I took down the first two and watched as Camaz took out three more. The elite had held their own as well. I began to look for Jacob. I could still smell his brother's scent vividly, so knowing they where brothers I would have no problem finding him. All of a sudden I was confronted by three hunters, two had swords, the other one had a bow and was pulling his arrow. I knew I had to take him out first. I ran at him, jumped into the air and came down, taking his head. I then took off after another. That man had a strong scent I knew. It was Jacob! I stopped and screamed, "Prepare for Death's Deliverer! You shall die for taking the life of my daughter!" I took him on in battle. He was very skilled, but I was very fast. He swung his sword at me. I dropped to the ground and rolled, coming up behind him. I swung my sword catching him across his back. He screamed out in pain and turned to face me. By then my eyes were glowing bright red with hatred. I leapt at him, knocking him to the ground. I raised my sword, bringing it down into his chest, driving it through his evil heart! I pulled my sword from his dead body, raised it in the air and said, "My beautiful Jade, for your death, I give you his!" I heard her sweet voice in my head, "Thank you, Mother!" I began to cry, the tears rolled down my face. Camaz ran over to me and asked if I was okay. I answered, "Oh, Camaz, I have heard our daughter thank me for avenging her death. Oh how I wish I could see her beautiful face again!" "I am so sorry you are grieving so, my darling. But just be happy she has seen you destroy the one that took her from us!" We went through the entire compound, destroying any hunters we come upon. Once we were done we set the place ablaze. But we made sure none of the forest was destroyed before we left. Once we were done we headed back to the airport and boarded the plane for Georgia.

CHAPTER 14

ALASKA, OH HOW I HATE THE COLD

It had been two years since we destroyed the compounds in Florida, Georgia and Ohio. We were heading to Alaska, god how I hated the cold! Once we had eradicated the vermin there we would be going back home to rest for a few days. Afterward we would be going into Canada. As I had said earlier we would not rest until all hunters had been wiped from the face of earth! I felt the plane touch down, so we got ready to disembark. We headed to a waiting SUV, loaded our equipment and headed to the area where we received intel on the Hunter's compound. Our friends in Alaska had set up a house for us and were awaiting our arrival. I was so ready for a hot bath, the cold had chilled me to the bone! We arrived at the house about an hour later, unload everything and went inside. We were greeted by Sonny and his mate Maria and shown to our quarters. The long nights there were perfect for hunting prey and

and hunters. Once we were inside of our quarters I told Camaz I was going to take a hot bath. He asked, "Would you like for me to join you, my queen?" "I would love that. I am so in need of a good bathing!" He ran the water for me and we stripped down. He got into the tub first and I followed, sitting between his legs. I leaned my head back onto his chest and he began to wash my arms. I felt him gently kiss me on my shoulder and go to the base of my neck. He licked all the way up to my earlobe, nicking it with one of his fangs, licking the blood as it dripped down. He ignited my passion deep within me. I turned around and straddled him, kissing him madly. I felt him enter me and I screamed out my pleasure. I began to ride him. With each stroke, he intensified my pleasure. I felt my heat ignite, my eyes rolled back in my head and I screamed his name over and over with each climax. I felt the urgency building in him. I screamed out, "Give it to me now!" I felt him explode inside of me. That caused the most intense orgasm yet. My whole body was rocked with delight. I brought him to my lips and kissed him madly. He stood up from the tub with himself still deep within me, carried me to the bed and collapsed on top of me. A few minutes later after we had caught our breath he said, "Woman, you never cease to amaze me! I think that was the most intense orgasm you have ever had!" I smiled up at him and said, "Only for you, my king!" He laughed, pulling me to him. We fell off to sleep, feeling the love between us stronger than ever. The next evening when we woke, we got dressed and headed to our meeting with Sonny and Maria. They gave us all of the intel on where the Hunters' compound was located. We loaded up all of our equipment and headed to the remote town of Moose Creek. There was only six hundred and fourth six humans in the whole town. But we knew there was a lot more there than had been reported. From the intel there were at least two hundred hunters in the compound. There was only a total of seventy-five of us. But I knew we could handle anything the hunters threw at us. But we had to take them by surprise, they could not know we were coming. We all took to the air, landing on top of the buildings in the compound. We began to look for hunters. I had my crossbow loaded and cocked to fire. The year before I had a special crossbow made for me. It fired four arrows before I have to reload. I had four more in my mouth. I watched as two men came from one of the buildings. I checked to make sure no one else was close by. I fired two of the arrows, taking out both men. I had sent Achilles and BamBam to remove the bodies so they would not be seen. We all leapt to the ground, entering separate buildings. Camaz, Vincent and myself entered a large building. I could hear the dogs coming up behind us. We came out into a room, quickly looking around for the hunters. I spotted three over to the left of us. I raised my crossbow and fired the other two arrows, taking two of them out. I heard the third man scream, "VAMPIRES!" The next thing I knew we were surrounded by about fifty hunters. I quickly reloaded the bow and fired, taking four down. But I didn't not have time to reload, we were being charged. I pulled my sword from behind and brought it around, making ready for battle. Everyone else had drawn their swords as well. I watched as the dogs went after the closest ones to them. I ran toward a man who was with a woman. She was not armed, so I assumed she was his mate. I went after her first, knowing he would come for me. Just as I reached her, he ran at me swinging his sword. I sidestepped him and he crashed into the wall behind me. He had hit so hard he was stunned for a moment. I leapt at him to deliver the killing blow. I suddenly felt something stab me in my back. I had never felt such pain! I turned to see who my attacker was. It was the woman who he was trying to protect. She was now coming at me with another silver spike. Just as she reached me I leapt up causing her to miss. I landed behind her, swung my sword and remove her head. I heard the man scream out and watched as he charged me. I pulled one of my daggers from it's sleeve and threw it at him, hitting him in the heart. He dropped to the ground dead. Suddenly I dropped down to my knees. The burn from the sliver was so intense that I began to shriek. Vincent ran over to me, pulled the spike from my back and did something amazing. He bit into his wrist and allowed his blood to flow into my wound. I felt the wound begin to close. I looked at him and said, "How is this possible? Only Camaz's blood can heal me, for we a are a bonded pair!" He smiled at me and said, "Bonded pairs are not the only ones that can heal, siblings can also heal." I looked at him puzzled and said, "That is impossible, we are not brother and sister!" "But that is where you are wrong. I was born four years after you. I am your brother! Our god, Cassandra came to me in a dream telling me of you and I was to find you. We are her champions!" I thought to myself, "Wow, I have a brother, how wonderful!" He reached for me, helping to my feet. I looked for Camaz but I did not see him anywhere. I called out to him in my mind. He answered, "I am not far, love. I have chased the last hunter to another room. As soon as I kill him I will be by your side." I told Vincent what Camaz had told me and there were no more hunters in the building. Just then Achilles came up to me. He had aarm in his mouth. He dropped it at my feet. I smiled down at him and said, "That's my good boy! You are my mighty Achilles!" He proceeded to lick my hand. A few minutes later Camaz came out of another room. I was so happy to see him. I ran to him and leaped into his arms. He said, "I have missed you to, my queen!" He hugged me to him. I cried out in pain from the wound in my back. He sat me down and turned me around. He said, "How is this wound healing on it's own, I have not bleed into it?!" I turned around smiling and said, "Camaz, I would like for you to meet my brother Vincent! We have the same parents in Canada." The only reply I got was "Wow!" He picked me up, carrying me out of the compound. Vincent and the dogs were right behind. We all took to the air, with Camaz carrying me. We flew back to our plane. Camaz carried me down to our sleeping area. He sat me down on the bed, offering me his neck. I bit down and his sweet blood began to flow. I felt my strength begin to return. I released his neck and pulled him to my lips.

CHAPTER 15

CANADA BOUND

We arrived back home the next evening. I was happy to be back

home, but the castle was so quite since everyone was gone. We

only have a few of our elite guards left. Astor survived the attack

and was our only council member at the time. Louisa survived the

attack in England, but she lost her husband and children. Right

after the attack she returned here for her recovery. Soon after she

began her own vendetta against the hunters. Mary Lou was also

there. The two of them had been traveling all over the world

helping with the eradication of the hunters. I was so happy to see

them again. I ran up and hugged both, telling them how much I had

missed them. After talking for a few minutes we all went to dress

for the hunt. We all hunted together that night. I could hardly wait,

I was starving! We went to our quarters with the dogs following

behind us. I went go to my closet to select my hunting outfit. I pulled on my skin tight leather pants and my leather lace up top. I finished it up with ankle length boots. Camaz looked at me and said, "My, my, looks like you have got your hunting spirit back. You look ravishing, my dear, good enough to eat!" "Yes I am finally feeling my love for the hunt coming back to me. As a matter of fact, I feel like running!" "That's my girl!" He pulled at my hand saying, "Let us go and enjoy the beautiful night, my love." We met up with everyone upstairs and left the castle. Once outside we took off running. I smiled to myself as I felt the wind on my face. God how I loved to run in the beautiful night! A few minutes later we arrived in town. We all leaped to the top of a high building and began to test the air for our prey. I picked up a wonderful scent a few streets over. There was enough to go around so we all leaped to the ground and headed toward the smell. We arrived at a run down house. I scented the house for innocents, there was none. It was time for the game! We sent Camaz, Vincent and Astor around to the back of the house. We then went up to the porch. I could tell there was three men and three women inside. They were in the living room and kitchen. I relayed this information to Camaz and us girls knocked on the door. A tall, skinny woman answered. We proceeded to tell her we were on the way to a party but our car had broken down and could we use her phone. She invited us in and told me she was going to go get her cell phone. There was another woman and two of the men in the living room. I watched as the men took us all in. One of them said, "Are you ladies going to some kind of costume party?" I smiled at him, but not enough to show my fangs. I said, "Yes sir, but our car has broken down. We are here on vacation but do not know anyone here to help us." The other man said, "God, you three are so beautiful! I hope you do not have anyone back home that will miss you!" He lunged for me, grabbing me. I allowed him to do this, my love for the game was now in full force. The other man grabbed Louisa. The woman pulled a gun on Mary Lou. The man holding of me said to the woman, "Call the others in here." She yelled out for the others in the kitchen. They came into where we were and I watched as the lust built in the other men eyes. At that point my blood lust had taken over. I signaled to Camaz the game was over and the party was on. They came in through the back of the house just as I broke the hold the man had on me, knocking him to the ground. In a matter of minutes they were all dead and growing cold. Oh what a feast that was! Soon after we were on our plane heading to Canada. Vincent, Louisa and Mary Lou were going with us. I could still remember deep down my birth parents, but I was sure they would not recognize me since I was back to my original self. When we touched down we were greeted by their elite guard and escorted back to the palace. As soon as we pulled up the memories of my childhood began to flood my mind, telling me Annie was still somewhere inside of me. We were taken directly to meet with the king and queen. As we walked into the room I seen my parents and my heart begins to sing. I watched as the truth of who I was appeared on their faces. My mother cried out, "Annie how is this possible? I do not see my beautiful daughter, but I know you are there!" I proceeded to tell them how our God sent me back to earth in her body so I could be reunited with my one true love. She came up to me and hugged me saying, "It does not matter that I can not see your face my daughter, but I know you are in there. I can smell your scent under hers." She said to me, "You are the one the hunters call Death's Deliverer aren't you?" "Yes ma'am, that I am, but your daughter is within me as well. When I seen both of you my heart soared! She gives me strength from within to handle anything. You have a very brave and loyal daughter!" We all talked for a few minutes more and we were escorted to our room. Those quarters would be ours until we had rid Canada of all the hunters. We unpacked and stored all of our weapons in the large closet. Camaz pulled me to him saying, "My queen, you have a good heart. I am so proud of how you put their minds at ease about their daughter!" "It was amazing, as soon as I saw them my mind was flooded with her memories. It made my heart sing for them!" He kissed me tenderly and asked, "Are you ready to hunt my love? Vincent told me he would show us all the good locations." I smiled up at him and said, "Yes, I am starving!" He laughed at what I said and we left the room to find Vincent. The girls were going with us as well. We had been told there were many vampire hunters through out the lands so we had dressed in our battle gear just to be safe. Vincent said, "Come, let us hunt!" He leapt into the air with all of us following him. Soon we were high above a large city looking down for prey. We had picked up the scent of our prey and landed on a building a few streets away. I sat on the ledge testing the air for hunters, just to be safe. I had not scented any so we leapt to the ground and headed off to where our dinner was. Suddenly I scented other vampires in the area. I stopped and said, "There is others of our kind here. They must be after the same prey." So we all leapt up to the top of the closest building and watched for the vampires. They came into view, there was two men and two women. We watched as they went into the house where our prey was located. Then we heard the screams begin. I looked at Camaz and said, "Should we leave and continue our hunt elsewhere, my love?" "Not just yet. I want to talk to these vampires to see if they want to join us in our quest." So we waited for them to come out of the house. We did not want to confront them all together so Vincent dropped down to the street and approached them. They talked for a few minutes and he signaled for us to come down. We leapt from the building and landed in front of them and the introductions were made. They were both mated couples. The first was James and Sarah, the second was Josh and Samantha, Sam for short. They, like us, were also hunting for the vermin. We invited them to join our group and they agreed. They like us had lost many family and friends. We all headed back to the castle. Along the way we hunted for our dinner. When we arrived at the castle and introduced our new friends to the king and queen. They were welcomed and taken to their quarters. We still had about four hours of darkness so we were going out again to search for the hunters. We had received information there was a group of hunters not far from from us so we took to the air in search of them. We arrived at a compound deep in a wooded area. I scented the air to see if there was any innocents we needed to get to safety, but from the scents they were all hunters. There was about fifth-teen to twenty of them in the compound. There were ten of us, so I thought the odds were in our favor. We all crept up closer to the compound and we saw four guards at the entrance. I pulled my crossbow from my side, loaded the arrows and took aim at the guards. I let the arrows fly, striking their targets. Once I had taken out all of the guards we ran from our cover and went into the compound. From the scents I could tell the remainder of the hunters were grouped together in one room. We creep down the hallway to the room, making sure we were not seen right away. I signaled to the ones behind us to make ready for battle. I pulled my sword from behind me, bringing it around. Camaz, Vincent and Astor had done the same. We signaled for the attack. We rushed the room, taking the hunters by surprise. I heard one man scream out, "My god, that is Death's Deliverer!" I took off running toward the man, leapt up into the air and came down in front of him with my eyes blazing red. I could see the horror on his face, for he knew what was coming. I swung my sword, catching him in the neck, severing his head from his body. I turned to face two more. I watched as one of the men reached for his gun. I quickly pulled one of my daggers and threw it at the hand reaching for the gun, hitting it. He screamed out in pain, dropping the gun. I rushed him, swung my sword, catching him across the chest. The blade dug deep, opening up his chest. He fell to the floor dead. Just as I began to turn toward the third man I felt a sharp pain in my chest. I looked down and there was an arrow. I began to feel the burn of the silver. I screamed out in pain and went down. The man who had fired the arrow was coming for me. I had to do something or he was going to kill me! As he began to pull back the bow again I reached for my other dagger and threw it at him, striking him in the neck. The blade had cut deep, he was bleeding profusely. The smell of his blood ignited my thrust, oh how I had wanted to feed on him. But I could not for he was a innocent. I laid there watching the last of that sweet blood leave his body. I felt the darkness began to pull at me, trying to take me away. I fought with all of my might, but I was not winning, I began to cry out Camaz's name over and over. I heard he's sweet voice saying, "I am here, my love, fight for me! I will get you back to the castle as quickly as I can." I felt myself being lifted up from the floor. I was then in his arms. I rested my head on his chest as he carried me out of the compound. The burn of the silver was intensifying, but I could tell the arrow was not as close to my heart as the arrow that ended my life. The darkness was all around me, pulling at me, saying it had came for me and would win this time. I began to scream over and over as I slipped deeper and deeper into the darkness. I began to pray to our god, asking to please not let me die. I had unfinished business on earth to do for her. I heard her say, "Wake up my child, I am not ready to bring you home to me!" I opened my eyes, screamed out in agony just as the healer removed the arrow from my chest. The tears began to run down my face, but they were not from the pain but the joy of being out of the darkness! I looked into Camaz's beautiful green eyes. I watched as the tears of joy ran down his face. I smiled at him and said, "Hello, my love!" He pulled me up into his arms and carried me down to our quarters. He laid me gently down onto the bed and kissed me tenderly. He broke our kiss and lifted my head to his neck saying, "Drink my love and get well for me!" I bit down gently and felt his blood flow into my mouth setting my soul on fire. I released my hold and said, "I was so afraid I would never look upon you face again, my love! My heart is singing right now with my joy!" He pulled me to his lips and kissed me like there would be no tomorrow.

CHAPTER 16

FREE OF THE VERMIN AT LAST

We had been hunting the vampire hunters for ten years and finally had rid the planet of the scum. We had met many new friends along the way and some had returned with us to Mexico. We had to rebuild our kingdom. We had lost so much it had been hard coming home. But I finally did not feel the hatred in my heart. It died with the last hunter I killed. But the sorrow for my children was still burned into my heart. I cried for them every night before I sleep. I constantly saw them in my dreams. We arrived home around 10pm, unload the plane and headed back to the castle. I had become very good friends with Candy, a woman I met in Scotland. She had came back to live with us. She had brought her husband William with her. Astor greeted us at the entrance of the cavern welcoming us back home. Camaz and Astor went off to discuss business. I took Candy's hand and said, "Come, my friend, I will show you and William to your quarters." I took them upstairs and into one of the spare rooms, leaving them to unpack. I walked down the hall to our quarters, closing the door behind me. Once behind the closed door I broke down crying. The halls that once was bounding with our children laughter were now silent. Oh how I missed them! I went into the bathroom and began to run myself a hot bath. A few minutes later Camaz came into the room and seen I had been crying. He came up to me, wiping the tears from my face. I looked up at him and smiled. "My beautiful queen, it beaks my heart to see you suffer so! How I wish I could stop your pain!" He took his clothes off and got into the tub with me. He began to wash me. I put my head on his chest and began to cry again saying, "Oh how I miss their laughter!" He touched my face and said, "I am so sorry, my love!" We just sat there holding each other. A few minutes later we were in our bed awaiting sleep. He had his arms around me, comforting me. He said, "My love, I know you cannot have children again, but if you wish we can look for a surrogate so we can have a child." I answered him, "No, my love, Cassandra said I would have children again, so I will wait. I trust in her totally." "As you wish, my love." After I fell off to sleep that night I dreamed of the future. I saw two small children playing in the courtyard. The boy had jet black hair and emerald green eyes, the girl had hair the color of corn silk and big beautiful blue eyes. My heart sang at the sight of them. I heard Cassandra's sweet voice saying, "I have felt your pain, my child, you are my champion and for ridding our world of the vampire hunters, behold your prize!" I looked at her with tears streaming down my face and said, "Oh thank you, they are so beautiful!" "I cannot say when, but soon you will feel the joy take hold of you." Then she was gone. I woke from the dream crying. He took me in his arms, telling me it was just a nightmare. I smiled at him and said, "No, it was not, it was the most beautiful dream I have ever had. I have looked upon our children before their births!" I told him everything Cassandra had told me. I could see the excitement in his eyes. Over the next few months we had gotten our kingdom back in order. We were currently recruiting for our new elite squad. There were many vampires, werewolves, demons and fairies there for the tryouts. As I watched the battles I notice a very fierce fairy, he reminded me of Dempie and his son. I watched as he quickly took down his opponent. He raised his sword to us. We stood and asked the mighty warrior his name, he replied, "I am Shawn, son of Dempie Jr and grandson of our mighty warrior Dempie Sr. We later found out his mother had hidden him away so the hunters would not find him. He said his father had spoken highly of us and from the time of his training he had always wanted to be apart of our elite squad. Camaz went over to Shawn, pulled his sword and tapped it on Shawn's left shoulder and then his right, proclaiming "Behold the mighty warrior and our head Elite guard Shawn!" Shawn bowed to us and thanked us. Camaz put him in charge of recruiting more fairies for our squad. We were seated again and continued with the games. There were two very fierce werewolves in the arena. We watched as they changed forms and went at each other. One was black the other white. I watched as the white wolf took his opponent down quickly. He had his massive paw at the other werewolf's throat, ready for the kill. He stood up, helping the other wolf to his feet. They both bowed to us. They shifted back into their human forms, standing before us. I asked the white wolf, "What is your name mighty warrior?" "My queen, my name is Devil, I am of the long tooth pack." I said, "Welcome mighty Devil to our elite squad!" "Thank you your highness, I swear before you and my king I will protect you with my life!" After the games we retired to our quarters to make ready for the hunt. Camaz took me into his arms and said, "Are you pleased with the choices I have made for our elite, my queen?" "Oh yes, very pleased!" Just then there came a knock at our door. Camaz went to the door and opened it. Astor told him he needed to speak with him. Camaz turned and said to me, "I will return soon, then we will hunt, my love." I smiled at him and said, "Hurry back, my king." They left the room after Camaz gave me a quick kiss. I went to my closet to pick out my hunting outfit. I knew how much Camaz loved to see me in my full black leather bodysuit, so I took it from the closet. I laid it on the bed and went to my dressing table. I began brushing my hair out. I looked at myself in the mirror. I saw the same young girl I had been so many years ago when I had met my one true love. I remembered back to our first meeting and how my heart had soared when I saw him. Oh how I loved him! He was my life and made me so very happy! I went over to the bed and began to put my bodysuit on. Just then Camaz returned, walked up to me and slowly pulled the zipper up my back. He kissed me on my neck and said, "Oh how I love you my beautiful queen. Do you know how happy you make me?" I turned around to face him and said, "God how you make my heart soar with you words. You are my heart, my one true love and I will love you for all of eternity!" He pulled me to his lips, kissing me tenderly. The following evening when we woke we got dressed for the hunt and went down to see if our guests would like to go with us. But they had left already to hunt. I told Camaz I felt like running that night, so we left the castle and sprinted into the forest. It was a warm summer night. I heard the crickets singing and an owl take flight. I watched him come down, scooping up his prey. Oh how I loved the sounds of the night! We stopped for a minute to test the air for our prey. We picked up on the scent of three not far away, but couldn't smell any innocents, so we took off in that direction. We leapt high up into a tree, their camp was right below us. There was two men and a woman having there dinner. I thought to myself, "Enjoy your last meal!" We dropped down from the tree. I landed on the woman and Camaz landed on one of the men. The third man took off running into the woods. I quickly stuck, draining the woman dry and took off running after the other man. My blood lust was on fire, driving me quicker and quicker toward my prey. I leapt in the air and came down, knocking the man to the ground. He was screaming for his life, but I did not hear him, the blood lust had taken me over completely. He was fighting me fiercely, but I knocked his hands away and struck, ripping his throat out. I drank and licked the blood as quickly as it left his body. When I was done I rolled off him panting. I could not figure out what the hell was wrong with me. I had never attacked with such viciousness! I was suddenly frightened. I called out to Camaz in my mind, he was at my side in seconds. I had tears rolling down my face. He pulled me up into his arms and said, "What is wrong? Why are you crying?" "Oh Camaz, I do not know what happened to me. The blood lust was so intense I attacked him as if I was some animal. I am so frightened, am I losing my mind? Has the madness returned to take me?" He said, "I do not think it is the madness, but we need to get you back to the castle to our healers to find out what has caused this!" He picked me up into his arms, leapt into the air and flew me back home. We went quickly to the healers and explained what had happened. Selina, our head healer asked, "My dear, was this the first time this has happened to you?"

I answer, "No, it has happened several times in the past but not as bad. It was like I was ravenous. I tore out his throat as if I was some animal!" She smiled and said, "My queen, it sounds like you are with child." I just stood there, I could not get the words out. Camaz spoke, "Are you sure? We did not think this was possible after the problems with Jade's birth!" "I am not for sure, all we can do is wait." So we left the healers and headed to our quarters. Once inside I sat down on the bed and began to cry. Camaz said, "Do not cry, my love, if it is not a child, it does not matter to me. All that matters to me is that I have you!" "Oh Camaz, do you think Cassandra's promise is coming to be? Will we have the beautiful children I have seen in my dreams?" "I do not know, my queen, all we can do is wait." About a week later while Camaz was away on business I was walking in the garden admiring the roses when I began to feel strange. I felt the pull and the joy. I was pregnant! I rushed into the castle and up to our quarters. I stood in front of my mirror and pulled up my top, looked at my belly and there I saw the small bump confirming what I already knew. I began crying tears of joy and thanked our god Cassandra for making my dreams come true. I heard her sweet voice in my head saying, "You are welcome, my child. You and Camaz deserve to be happy again so I have granted your wish." I smiled at what she had said and I began to think of a way to surprise Camaz when he returned the following evening. I called the restaurant where we met, had our 40th anniversary and made reservations for 9pm the next evening. I went into town shopping. I went to our jeweler and looked for the perfect gift. I found a beautiful silver baby spoon. I knew our child would never use the spoon, but it was the perfect way to let him know I was with child. I had the shop keeper put it into a black velvet box, paid him and left for home. That night I went hunting, Achilles, BamBam and Devil were with me for protection. I had become great friends with Devil. He was such a great guy and funny as hell! We sat atop a building testing the air for our prey. I picked up on a scent and dropped down to the street below. I began following the wonderful smell. My protectors were right behind me, keeping to the shadows. I spotted my dinner and began walking up to the man. As I walked past him I watched the lust build in his eyes. I heard him began to follow me. I loved a good chase, but I also loved the lore game. I turned into a alleyway knowing it was a dead end. I stopped and turned around to go back out, but he was in front of me. He attacked me, pushing me up against the brick wall. I began to scream, but he put his hand over my mouth. He put a knife to my throat and said, "If you scream I will slit your throat!" He turned me around, facing the wall, lifted my skirt and I heard him begin to unzip his pants. I smiled to myself. He then tried to spread my legs apart. I stopped him from doing it and with lightning speed I reversed our positions. I slammed him into the wall. He said, "How in the hell did you do that?" I smiled at him, baring my fangs and said, "Asshole, I am a vampire. I am a hundred times stronger than you and you are my dinner for tonight!" I slammed his head to the side and struck, sinking my fangs deep into his neck. I felt his sweet blood begin to flow, setting my killing instinct off. I ripped his throat out, spit it to the ground and began lapping the gushing blood from the open wound. God he was so sweet!

CHAPTER 17

MY BIG SURPRISE

The following morning around 4am Camaz returned home. I ran to him and jumped into his arms. "Welcome home, my one true love!" He smiled and said, "It is good to be home, my queen. Oh how I have missed not holding you in my arms!" He pulled me to his lips, kissing me ever so gently. I asked if he had fed and he said, "Yes, but I have a hunger only you can quench, my love!" He carried me up to our quarters. He sat me down on the bed and began to undress me. I stared into his beautiful emerald green eyes and my heart soared! I so wanted to tell him right there, but I would wait until the next evening. I watched as he removed his clothes, his manhood standing at full attention. I felt the burn begin way down low. I knew I was not far enough along yet to do harm to the baby, so I pulled him down to me and begun to kiss him slowly. I felt my need for him ignite to a inferno. I moaned, "Oh how I have missed your beautiful body, you have set my soul on fire! My need is great, my love!" I felt him enter me. I screamed out his name as he began to thrust. I told him over and over how much I loved him. We both exploded at the same time, riding the climax to it's end. I laid there feeling the shivers of my pleasure wash over me. He rolled off of me, pulling me to his chest. There I fell asleep with a smile on my face, for tomorrow he would learn we were expecting a child again. The following evening when we arose he asked me where I would like to hunt. I told him I wanted to go somewhere first before we hunted. He asked, "Where would my queen like to go?" I answered, "I have been wanting to go to our restaurant so I can see the beautiful nightshade, can we go, my love?" "Anything my queen's heart desires, I will provide!" I announced, "I feel like running!" So out the castle into the woods we ran. We arrived at the back of the restaurant and went to where the nightshade was in bloom, the smell was so wonderful. He pulled me into his arms, kissing me tenderly. I smiled at him and said, "Oh how I remember the night when you kissed me for the very first time. You stole my heart that night and I never looked back!" He smiled at me and said, "You made me the happiest man on earth when you told me you wanted to spend the rest of eternity with me, my queen!" He pulled me back to his lips, kissing me passionately. I broke our kiss, reach into my pocket and pulled out the black box. I handed it to him smiling. He said, "What is this, my queen? It is not our anniversary yet." "Open it and you will find out!" He opened the box, looked down at the silver baby spoon. I watched as the joy lit up his face. He asked, "My love, are you telling me you are with child?" "Yes, my love, I am!" He pulled me to him and swung me around and around, telling me how happy he was. I began to cry saying, "I knew if I waited our god would fulfill my wish!" He picked me up and leapt into the air. I asked, "Where are we going, my love?" "Home." "But we have not hunted yet, I am starving!" He laughed and said, "Always thinking with your stomach!" "But my dear, you have to remember

I am eating for two!" That night, after the hunt, when we were in our quarters, he ran me a hot bath. He carried me into the bathroom, stripped me and striped himself. He placed me in the tub, in front of him and began to wash my body. When he reached my belly he could feel the small bump. I could not see it, but I could feel the smile on his face. After our bath he carried me out to the bed and laid me down. He started to kiss me, starting at my neck, then all the way down to my belly. He began to talk to our child, telling him or her how happy the child's mother had made him. He kissed his way back up to my lips and said, "I love you my beautiful queen, my heart sings for you and our child!" With his words I felt my heart take wings and fly. That night I dreamed of the two beautiful children Cassandra had shown me. It had been three weeks since we found out about the baby. I had grown heavy with the child, heaver than with my prior children. I stood in front of the mirror looking at my swollen belly. Camaz came up to me from behind, put his arms around me at my belly and said, "My god, you are so beautiful, my love you are absolutely glowing!" I answered, "I cannot wait to see our child! Oh how I yearn to have a child in this castle again. I so miss our children!" "As I, my love, but just remember what Cassandra told you, all of our children are with her and happy!" "I know, my love, I just wish I could look upon there sweet faces again." He turned me around, hugging me to him. We got dressed and went down to the holding cells for our meal. He did not want me out hunting so close to the birth. As I feed, something strange happened. I felt the pull telling me it was time for the birth. But I was only into the third week. I cried out for Camaz, he came running into the cell and asked, "What is wrong?" I looked at him with tears in my eyes and said, "I can feel the pull of birth, something is wrong, it is to soon!" He picked me up quickly running from the room. We headed to the healers to find out what was wrong. I was checked out by the healers and told the child was coming. I was so afraid I was going to lose the baby! I cried out, "No, no, please I cannot bare to lose another child, my heart will break completely! Camaz please do something!" I felt the urge to push. I screamed out, "The baby is come, please, please do something!" Suddenly the child was out. Camaz smiled at me and said, "It is a boy! He is perfect and healthy, my love, he is the child of your dreams!" He handed the baby to me. I looked down at the most beautiful child I had every seen. He had Camaz's black hair and emerald green eyes. He so reminded me of Camazotz! Then something strange happened. I felt the urge to push again. I screamed out, "Something is wrong! I feel the pull again, what is wrong with me!" The healer smiled and said, "My queen, there is another child coming!" "What! Another? Are you kidding me?" I watched as Camaz's eyes lit up with his joy. I pushed one more time and our second child was out. I watched as the tears of joy ran down my beloved's face. He proclaimed "Behold, my love, the daughter of your dreams!" He handed me the baby. She was as I pictured her, with hair the color of corn silk and the most beautiful blue eyes I had ever seen. I began to cry my own tears of joy, thanking Cassandra over and over in my mind. I heard her sweet voice, "You are welcome, my child. Love them as you have with all of your other children, for they shall be the last. As a royal female you can only have four in your lifetime." I thanked her again. After the healers had finished with me Camaz carried me in one arm and our babies in the other to our room, laying us down onto the bed. He smiled at me and said, "Thank you, my love they are now my heart as well!" He told me he was going down to the holding cells to get their first meal and would be back soon. After he left I stared down at our beautiful children, my heart soared. For now I am going to put my pen down. But I promise I will be back to tell you more of my wondrous life!

CHAPTER 18

LOVE IN THE MOONLIGHT

It has been two years since I last wrote in my diary. We had been enjoying the children and each other. We had named the children after our lost ones Camazotz and Jade. They were the spitting image of their lost brother and sister. We had told them of all their brothers and sisters and how we lost them to the vampire hunters two years before. After the twin's birth our god Cassandra came to me in a dream, letting me know she had sent the souls Jade and Camazotz back to us in the twins. She told me it was our reward for ridding the planet of the vermin. I still longed to see the faces of my other children, lost family and friends. But I knew they were all happy and safe with Casandra. It was a beautiful summer night. We were running through the forest. Oh how I loved to run! That night Devil had came with us. As promised, he had stayed by my side, protecting me with his life. He was so funny, god how he made me laugh! As we ran, Devil tried to catch us, but we were just to fast. He yelled, "Hey, how am I going to protect you, my queen if you are going to out run me all of the time. Now get back here and let me do my job!" I busted out laughing, misjudge my steps, tumbling to the ground, laughing all the way. They both ran up to me with Devil saying, "Talk about a clumsy vampire!" Camaz laughed, "Tell me about it, the woman has two left feet!" I looked up at them and said, "Ha, ha, very funny, now help me up!" They both reached for me, but I had other plans. I yanked both of them down to the ground and said, "So now, what was you saying about me being a clumsy vampire!" We all busted out laughing, staring up at the beautiful night sky. The moon was full that night and the stars were shining brightly. I sighed saying, "Oh how I love the beautiful night! Thank you, my love for giving me this wondrous life!" "It was my pleasure my beautiful queen!" We got up and quickly took off running again. We slowed enough so Devil could keep up with us. All of a sudden I picked up the scent of werewolves. I stopped dead in my tracks and tested the air again. I counted four in all. I was not afraid as I use to be, for I knew both of my protectors were with me. I said, "The smell of werewolf is very strong here, I have scented four of them." Devil said, "Yes, there are three males and a female. Shall we go see what they are up to?" I smiled saying, "Lead the way my protector!" We all laughed and Camaz took my hand as we walked toward where I had scented the werewolves. We came to a clearing, spotting the werewolves. We crouched low, watching as they seemed to be up to something. One of the males had the female on the ground, the other two were holding her down. It looked as if they were going to rape her. I felt the hatred began to build within me. I began to stand up, but Devil stopped me and said, "No, we cannot interfere. This is her passage into the pack." "But Devil they are going to rape her, I cannot allow this!" "If we interfere, she will be shunned by the pack, you must allow this to happen!" "Then we need to leave this place for I cannot stand by and do nothing!" I leapt into the air, heading away from the horrible scene. I was so angry with Devil I did not even want to speak with him at the time. Camaz had joined me and said, "I am sorry you are so angry, my dear, but you have to understand that werewolves have there on rules, they must be followed!" "I just could not stand by and watch that poor girl get raped! It has been many years since my rape, but it is still burned into my memory!" By then I had begun crying. The blood tears were flowing down my face. He pulled me into his arms, setting down on the ground and said, "You are breaking my heart, my queen, how I hate to see you suffer! You have such a good heart, but there is nothing we can do for the girl, I am sorry." He pulled me into his arms, raised my face to him, wiping away my tears. He pulled me to his lips, kissing me tenderly. Devil joined us and said, "I am sorry, my queen but we cannot interfere with pack business, the rules are strictly enforced. If we had done anything I would have been challenged by the pack master." "It is okay Devil, I do not blame you. But I think the rule needs to be changed! In our coven if a female is rape it is her right to kill her attacker! I know because it happen to me a long time ago and he paid with his life by my hands." He said, "I am so sorry, my queen, I did not know." "It is alright Devil, let us not speak of it again. Shall we hunt, I am starving!" We all took off running until we reached the city. We leapt to the top of a building and began testing the air for our prey. I suddenly picked up on a scent. It was strange, not human, but not vampire either. I asked Camaz, "Do you know this scent? I have never smelled anything like it!" "It is unfamiliar to me as well dear." We watched in amazement as the creature came from the shadows. It was about five feet long, with long flowing fur the color of gold. It's eyes were glowing bright green. I looked closer at the beast and it clicked., the creature looked like a lynx. But I could also tell it is more than that. I said to the men, "It looks like a lynx but it is supernatural as well!" We watched as it stalked up the street. Suddenly I caught the smell of something evil. His blood was calling to me, but the creature was also stalking the man. I told the men to stay put, so not to frighten the creature. I leapt from the building, heading toward the creature. I had drawn my sword just to be safe. Suddenly the beast turned, it had scented me. I watched as it started to charge me. I held up my hand and said, "I mean you no harm beast, like you I am hunting the evil one." The beast spoke in a female voice, "This is my meal, go away!" "As you wish, but I just wanted to introduce myself. I am Queen Anne of the vampire kingdom. We are looking for all manor of supernaturals to join our coven. If you are interested we would like to speak to you after your hunt." She said, "I am Sonja, I am of the lynx pride. I would love to talk with you, shall me meet in the woods just east of here when I have finished my meal. I have your scent, so I will be able to find you." "That would be great Sonja, I will await you. But like you I am hungry, so I will leave you to your meal." I leaped back to the top of the building where the men were waiting. I told them we would meet her in the woods after the hunt. I tested the air to see if there were other evils in the area. I soon picked up a scent so we leaped to the ground, running off in the direction of the wonderful smell. We had all feed and were in the woods awaiting Sonja. About twenty minutes later she walked up to us, but was in human form. God she was stunning. Her long brown hair hung down past her waist and her eyes were the color of jade. I introduced her to Camaz and Devil and ask if she would like to accompany us back to the castle. She agreed and changed back into her lynx form. Devil shifted as well and we all took off running into the beautiful night. A few minutes later we arrived at the castle. I called to Maria to come and show our guest to the guest quarters. We told Sonja we would see her the following evening. We said good night to Devil and went to our quarters. We went to check on the twins first, they had already fed and were awaiting sleep. We went into their rooms, kiss them good night and told them how much we loved them. We left going to our room. As I was undressing he asked, "So what are you thinking, my dear? Adding her to the elite squad?" "I think she would make a great addition to the elite. We do not have anyone like her and maybe she will recruit more of her kind. We can always use good warriors since we are still having problems with the ghouls!" "So true, my love. Would you prefer a bath or shower tonight?" I thought for a minute and answered, "I would love a hot bath, as long as you join me, my king!" He smiled at me and said, "The pleasure is all mine, my queen!" He went into the bathroom to run our bath. While he was doing that I went to my dressing table, sat down and began to brush out my hair. I heard him approach. I smiled to myself and felt him take the brush from me. He pulled me up into his arms, bringing me to his lips. He kissed me slowly at first, then intensified the kiss. I felt the fire began to build way down low. He picked me up, carrying me into the bathroom, never breaking our kiss. He sat down in the tub. By then my soul was ablaze with my hunger for him. He broke our kiss and began to kiss down my neck, driving me wild with pleasure. He reached the base of my neck and licked all the way back up. I grunted out my pleasure. He

said, "Oh how I love when you do that! It sets my soul on fire!" He
pulled me back to his lips, kissing me with all within him. I felt his
hands grab my buttocks, raising me to him. As he entered me I
threw back my head screaming out his name over and over. I
brought my head back down and looked into those burning emerald
green eyes. I could see the lust building in those eyes. I began to
rotate my hips to each of his thrusts. He was moving faster and
faster. I could tell we were both close, so I began to lick his neck
and bit. He screamed out his passion, biting me. We both exploded,
riding the pleasure of what we were feeling. I looked him in the
eyes and said, "God how you please me in all ways, my king!" He
smiled at me and said, "As do you, my queen. I have never felt
such passion in all of my 900 years! You are my one true love and
there can be no other!" With those words I felt my heart take wings
and fly! I pulled him to my lips, kissing him tenderly. He stood
from the tub with me in his arms and carried me to our bed. I
cuddled into his arms, falling off to sleep knowing the man was my

heart and I would love him for all of eternity! The following evening when we woke we went up to talk to our new friend Sonja. She was in the living room with Devil, they seamed to be getting along fabulously. We walked into the room and said hello to both of them. We told Sonja about our elite squad and we would like her to join. She said, "I will have to think about it for a bit, if that is alright with you. I will also need to take it up with the leader of my pride." "Take as long as you wish, the invitation will always be open to you." Shortly after she left to head back to her pride. I watched as Devil watched her leave. I could see a sparkle in his eyes. I went up to him and asked, "Do I see interest in those eyes? Does she appeal to you my brave Devil?" He smiled saying,"She is so beautiful! I feel my heart sing when I see her!" "You need to tell her how you feel, she may feel the same for you." "But she is a lynx and I am a wolf how will that ever work out!" "Devil I was once human, but when I met Camaz he made my heart sing. I had never wanted anyone as much as I did him. If you find your soul mate then it is meant to be." "I will speak to her when she returns, letting her know how I feel. I hope she feels the same!" Camaz pulled at my hand and said, "I am quite hungry, my love, shall we hunt?" I smiled at him and said, "Catch me if you can!" I took off running like the wind out into the beautiful summer night. I could hear him behind me, so I sped up even more and as usual I misjudged my steps and went down laughing. He stopped in front of me and said, "Woman, you simply amaze me, to be so graceful and clumsy at the same time!" I reached up, pulling him down on top of me and said, "Come here!" He looked down into my eyes and my heart soared for him. He was stunningly handsome, his body would put any man to shame and he was all mine for all of eternity! I placed my hand on his face and said, "Do you have any idea how much I love you! You are mine as I am yours!" He pulled me to his lips, showing me just how much he knew I loved him. A few minutes later we were up running again like the wind. We were deep in the woods. I had scented three evils off to the east so we were headed that way. We reached a clearing and leapt into a tall tree. We sat there looking down at the men. I tested the air for innocents but couldn't smell any. I smiled at Camaz and said, "Oh goodie, we do not have to rescue anyone! Shall we my dear!" We both leapt from the tree, landing in front of the men. They were startled momentary, but then started screaming, running off in different directions. I took off after the one who had run to the left, Camaz was in pursuit of the man who went to the right. The third man was running with the one I was after. I pulled one of my daggers, throwing it at one of the men, he went down hard. I leapt at the other, taking him to the ground. I slammed his head to the side, struck and began to drink. His sweet blood had set my soul on fire. I drained him dry and went after the other man. The dagger had dug deep into his back and he was bleeding out. He looked up at me and said, "Please help me, I am dieing!" I smiled down at him, showing my fangs and said, "Why should I help you? You are nothing but a low life murder!" I struck, sinking my fangs deep into his neck. The blood began to flow and I drank him down. I stared up at the beautiful night sky while I waited for Camaz. A few minutes later he arrived at where I was, reached for me, pulling me to my feet and said, "Well, my queen, have you had your fill for the night?" "Yes, I am quite full, they were both so evil!" He laughed and said, "Come, let us go home." We took off running toward home.

CHAPTER 19

SONJA'S RETURN

It had been a month since we had met Sonja, but we had yet to hear from her. One evening we were out hunting when I picked up her scent. I ran toward where she was, but stopped. She was not alone. She had four others of her kind with her, two male and two female. We went up to them, saying hello. She introduced us to the others. The two males were Reggie and Jason, the two females were Star and Catherine, Cat for short. We invited them all back to the castle. As we were heading back home I thought to myself, "Boy is Devil going to be surprised!" Sonja was all he had talked about since she left. When we arrived at the castle I told Maria to make rooms up for our guests. Just then Devil entered the room. I watched as his eyes lit up when he saw Sonja. He walked up to her, took her hand, kissing it and said, "Welcome back, Lady Sonja! I am so glad you have decided to return!" I watched as she smiled at him and thanked him. I had seen the same sparkle in her eyes as I had seen in Devil's. I was so happy! Maria came in letting us know all of the rooms were ready for our guests. She escorted them up to the rooms. But Sonja had stayed behind, talking to Devil. He asked, "Would you like to go for a walk with me in the gardens?" She smiled at him and said, "I would love to!" They said their good nights to us and left. I turned to Camaz and said, "Oh Camaz, I could see the sparkle in her eyes, I think we are going to have a mated couple soon!" He laughed and said, "My matchmaker queen!" He pulled at me and said, "Shall we retire to our quarters my love, I have something to give you!" I thought to myself, "Oh goodie, I just love the gifts he gives me!" Once we were in our room, I begin to undress. I went to the bed, crawling up, showing all for him to see. Suddenly he was behind me. I felt him enter me and I cried out my pleasure. He had his hands on my hips and was gliding himself, every so gently, into me. As he pulled back I screamed out his name. He thrust again, sending me over the edge. I locked myself down around him, causing him to yell out his pleasure. He began to stroke quicker and quicker. I was so close I felt as though I was going to explode. He was kissing my neck and I felt him bite. That sent me over the cliff and into the abyss. I screamed over and over with each drop of blood he took. Suddenly I felt him let go deep inside of me. He was licking my neck were he had bitten me. That sent tiny shivers of delight down my spine. He collapsed on top of me. We just laid there enjoying our ecstasy. He rolled off of me to his side of the bed. I rolled over to face him. I smiled and said, "Wow that was amazing! I think that was the strongest orgasm you have every given me! My love you complete me in all ways!" He pulled me to his chest and said, "As do you, my queen. I love you totally heart and soul!" I fell off to sleep in his loving arms. When we woke the next evening we went to meet with our new friends. We had discussed making Sonja the head of our new elite Lynx squad and had agreed, if she is willing. We met them upstairs and told them we would be taking them to Cristos to our elite squad headquarters. I asked to speak with Sonja alone. We went off to the library and I said, "Sonja we have discussed making you the head of our new elite Lynx squad and would like to know if you want the position" She smiled at me and said, "It would be an honor, my queen!" "Great, lets us go tell the others." We meet up with the others and told them the good news. Everyone congratulated her and we left for Cristos. Devil was with Sonja, they had shifted into their beast forms, taking off into the night. I was so happy for them! We arrived at the headquarters about twenty minutes later. Stantos greeted us and we all went to the war room. Everyone was already in attendance so we made the announcement about our new group and we were adding them to the elite squad. We introduced them one by one. I announced, "We have put Sonja in charge of the lynx squad, she will only take orders from us, is this understood?" They all yelled out, "Yes, my queen!" Stantos had their quarters prepared so I asked Devil to take them to the quarters so they could get settled in. A few minutes later Stantos told us he had some disturbing news. We went over and sat down at the table. He said, "Sires, we have just received Intel there is a problem with the ghouls. They have been killing in our lands. They have a new leader and from the reports he is very powerful. We sent a scout out to find out what was going on, but he has not returned. I fear he has been destroyed." We told Stantos to make everyone ready for battle and we were going back to the castle to get our battle gear. We quickly left the compound. We arrived at the castle and headed to our quarters to retrieve our gear. But before we got to our room we stopped to check on the twins. They were 2 ½ by then. They had grown so much. Soon they would come of age and be proclaimed adults. I was in Jade's room. She was listen to music. She smiled at me and said, "Good evening Mother, I am so happy you are home." I went up to her, hugging her to me and said, "Thank you my beautiful daughter, but we will not be home long. We have a problem we must take care of. I need you to promise me you will stay close to the castle and not hunt alone." "I promise Mother, please come back to me safe!" "I will." I kissed her on the cheek and left the room. Next I went to Camazotz's room. I relayed the same information to him and kissed him goodnight. He asked, "Mother, why can I not go with you? I have trained well with father. I could help!" "Son, you are the future of our kingdom and with that comes responsibilities. You must stay here, guard the castle and your sister." "Very well Mother." I told him goodnight and left his room, heading to our quarters. Camaz was already inside getting everything together. I went to my closet, pulled out my black body suit and put it on. Camz came over and zipped me up. I placed my sword on my back and my daggers on my arms. I pulled the crossbow from the closet and grabbed the arrows. The fear for the ghouls was still within me, but I could not show fear or Camaz would make me stay behind. He asked, "Are you ready, my love?" "Yes, let us go so we can take care of this problem!" We left the castle, leapt into the air and headed back to Cristos. When we arrived at the headquarters everyone was ready. We all took off to where the ghouls had been seen. Devil and Sonja were right by our sides in their beast form. We arrived in a clearing, duck down because there was at least one hundred ghouls in the camp below. We were going to send our lynx squad out to investigate. I knew the ghouls had never seen them before. Sonja lead the way. I scanned the group, looking for the leader. I knew he was the one we had to take out. Suddenly I spotted him. He was huge and the ugliest thing I had ever seen. He was over six feet tall, had all that horrible greenish skin and red eyes. My fear for the ghoul was growing inside of me, but I could not let Camaz see my fear or he would have made me stay behind. I refused to leave his side. We called the charge and rushed down toward the ghouls. We watched as they drew their swords, reading for our attack. I pulled my crossbow around, loaded the arrows and started firing. I took down four and reload, firing again. I was getting closer to where I had seen the leader. But there was so many of them it was hard to find him. Camaz and Devil had not left my side but they were in battle with the four ghouls, so it was hard to keep tabs on me. Suddenly I spotted the leader. He was fighting with our fairy squad and he was winning! I rushed toward him not thinking about my safety. I pulled my sword from it's sheath and brought it around. He saw me coming and charged toward me I leapt just in time, causing him to miss me. I dropped to the ground, rolled and came up swinging. I caught him across the chest, but it was not a killing blow. He slammed into me, knocking me to the ground. I had lost my sword, so I went for my daggers. He grabbed both of my arms and said, "Oh no you don't, little vampire!" I became really pissed! I began to fight, trying to free my arms, but he was just to strong. I watched him rear back to bite me. I screamed out in terror, then he was gone. Devil had rammed into him, knocking the ghoul off of me. I watched as they battled. My mighty Devil had the ghoul down on the ground and was getting ready to rip it's throat out. Out of the corner of my eye I seen two ghouls running at them. I thought, "Oh shit!" I leaped to my feet, grabbing my sword and ran toward them. I leapt in front of them, swung and took the first one's head. But the other ghoul had time to come around behind me. All of a sudden I felt intense pain in my back. I thought to myself, "Oh god, the ghoul has bitten me!" I screamed out Camaz's name as I fell to the ground. I began to pray to our god, "Cassandra, please, please, do not let me plunge into madness. I could not go through it again!" I watched as my love ran up to me and took a protective stance as the ghoul came for me again. He swung and I watched as the ghoul's head left his body. He turned to me and said, "I heard you scream out that you have been bitten! Please tell me this is not so!" I told him what happened, but the monsters had not come for me yet. He turned me over to check for bite marks. He gasps and said, "Thank god! You have not been bitten. But you have a dagger in your back!" He pulled the dagger out. I screamed out in pain as it came out. He bit his wrist, pouring his healing blood into the wound. I felt wound begin to seal. A few minutes later I was feeling better. Camaz helped me to my feet and we went to check on the others. We went to where Devil was standing, he said, "I was so afraid he was going to get you, my queen! I took him down but he got away. He ran off that way." He pointed to the east. I said to both of them, "We must go quickly. We cannot allow him to get away!" I took off running and was joined by Camaz, Devil, Sonja and Stantos. We began to track the ghoul by his scent. Suddenly I spotted him off in a clearing. I screamed out and took off after him. He saw me coming, raised his sword, making ready to do battle with me. The others were right behind me. I leapt at the ghoul, knocking him to the ground, I raised my sword and ready for the killing blow. He looked up at me with those burning red eyes and said, "Do as you must, little vampire, but just know there are many more of my kinsman and they will be coming for all of you!" I brought the blade down, taking his head. I wiped the blood off of my sword and placed it back in it's sheath behind my back. Camaz came up to me and said, "My mighty warrior queen, you are amazing!' "Thank you, my love, but our work is not done. We need to get back to the compound to make ready for the search to find the others." We all helped our wounded, taking them back to the compound. We called a meeting of our war council. Once everyone had gathered, we went over our plans. Camaz announced, "We will start at their home in the graveyard and we will not rest until we have cleared our lands of all ghouls!" All of our warriors cheered for their king. Daylight was coming, so we had to make ready for sleep. All of our daytime protectors would be here to protect us in case there was an attack. We said goodnight to everyone and went deep below the compound where our quarters were located. Once inside he said, "My queen, you were so brave today! I am so proud of you!" "It is you that makes me feel brave, my love. I feel as though I could take on the world as long as you are by my side!" He pulled me to him, kissing me tenderly. We went to the bed and made ready for sleep. We would have a very hard night tomorrow evening. There were thousands of ghouls under the graveyard. That night I dreamed. I saw our god Cassandra. She told me, "It is so good to see you so happy, my child. But I must warn you, with this battle will come great loss. Keep Camaz close to you,

for he is the only one that can protect you from what is coming!"
With that she was gone. I awoke crying. I felt Camaz pull me to him
and he asked, "What is wrong my love? Why are you crying? Have
you had a nightmare?" He wiped the tears from my face. I look up at
him and said, "It was not a nightmare, but our god did come to me in
the dream. She has warned me to stay close to you during the battle,
that only you can protect me." "If this is so, then you will stay here
with the children. I cannot have you in harms way!" "No, I will not
stay behind while you put your life on the line. I have sworn to
protect you and I will, even if it means my life!" He kissed me
gently and said, "As you wish. But I will not leave your side for
anything. Do you understand? I cannot lose you again!" I answered,
"Yes." Dusk was almost upon us, so we got up, dressed and made
ready for the battle. I had pulled my hair up high in a ponytail so I
would have easy access to my sword. I had placed my spare daggers
in my boots. I watched as my mighty warrior dressed in his gear. His
huge muscles rippled as he was placing his weapons on his body,

god I could have watched him forever! We called Achilles and BamBam into the room. We told them they were to go back to the palace to protect the children with their lives. They barked out they understood and took off heading back to the castle. We left our quarters going up to the war room. Everyone was there and ready. We left the compound, heading to the graveyard. Devil and Sonja were right by our sides in their animal forms. After about an hour we came up on the graveyard. The smell of ghoul was very strong there. We knew where the entrance was from the last time we where there. I could still remember the night like it was yesterday. I could still feel the cold blade cutting into my throat, sending shivers down my spine. But I had to be careful, I couldn't show the fear I was feeling. We went to the entrance and descended into the darkness. We came out into a large cavern where the ghouls lived. They were everywhere, but we were ready for them. We rushed in with our swords drawn, taking them out as we went. I watched as Devil took one down and ripped out it's throat. The same had happened with

Sonja. Suddenly we were charged by at least a dozen. Camaz pushed

me behind him, making ready for the attack. But I was ready for

them. I had my crossbow in front of me, letting four arrows fly,

reloaded, taking out four more. Just as I was ready to reload I felt

something strike my arm I had the crossbow in. I screamed out,

dropping the bow. I looked and there was a dagger in my arm. The

silver was burning badly. I yanked the dagger from my arm, throw it

at the ghoul in front of me, striking it in the heart. He went down.

Luckily I had not been struck in my sword arm. I reached around

me, grabbed the hilt of my sword, and brought it forward. We

charged the remaining three in front of us. I swung, catching one of

them across the chest. He screamed out in pain and started to back

away. Camaz had caught the second one across the neck, removing

it's head. But the third was on me like lightning, knocking me to the

ground. I had lost my sword so I went for my dagger. I brought it

around to strike the beast, but he knocked it from my hand. I had to

get him off of me, before he could bite. I brought my knees up into his chest, tossing him off. I jumped to my feet and ran for my sword. I reached down, grabbed it and brought it around. But before I could strike I watched the ghoul fly through the air. It was Sonja. She leapt on the beast and ripped it's throat out. Camaz was at my side helping me to my feet. I raised my sword to Sonja, honoring her for her bravery. We went deeper into the ghouls' lands. There were so many of them, but we were holding our own. We knew there was another leader somewhere in there along with their council. We needed to find them all and take them out. I had my crossbow in front of me, ready to fire if we were attacked. Our elite had taken out most of the ghouls in front of us, so we pushed on into the heart of their lair. Soon we came upon a building that looked like it could be where the leader and council were located. It was very well guarded. I raised my bow and let the first four arrows fly, taking out the guards in front of the entrance. Suddenly more came rushing from inside and attacked us. I had reloaded the crossbow. I took aim and took out four more. Camaz, Devil, Sonja and Stanos were in battles with the ghouls. I took off running into the building without thinking

about Cassandra's warning. I came out into a large room. I saw their

leader, he was sitting with the council. I pulled my bow back, ready

to fire on them when I was struck from behind. Suddenly I was in

the darkness. But as quick as I went into the darkness I was back in

the light. I opened my eyes to a horrible sight. The leader was

standing over me. I had been tied down to something. I screamed out

to Camaz in my head, letting him know I had been capture and to

hurry, the leader was going to kill me! Suddenly I heard Camaz's

sweet voice yelling, "Get away from her ghoul. If any harm comes to

my wife I will tear you to pieces myself!" The ghoul laughed and

said, "Come, vampire king, try and take her from me!" Camaz leapt

at the ghoul, swung his sword, but missed. The ghoul was very

quick. I watched in horror as the ghoul swung his sword at Camaz.

He ducked causing the ghoul to miss as well. Then they began their

dance of death. I had never seen a ghoul with the skills that one had.

He met Camaz's blade with his own over and over. Suddenly the others enter the room, one of the ghoul's council was quickly up and at me with his sword to my throat and yelled, "Stop or I will kill her! Her life is in the hands of her husband, only he can free her!" I felt the cold sliver on my neck. Suddenly all of the memories of that horrible day flooded my mind. Thinking I had been lost to the darkness forever, never to see my beloved again. The anger began to build within in me. I could feel the heat as my eyes began to change to burning red hatred. The ghoul began to back away from me. I could see the fear in his eyes. I watched the leader strike Camaz in the chest and he went down. He was bleeding very badly. The leader raised his sword to deliver the killing blow. I screamed out in rage, "I. Have. Had. Enough!" I felt my whole soul ignite with my anger. The next thing I knew my entire body was ablaze. The fire burned through my bindings. I stood up and turned toward the ghoul. I watched as the horror reached his face. But he was very brave. He screamed out, running at me with his sword. I reached behind me pulling my sword in front of me. My sword burst into flames as well.

He swung at me and I meet his blow with my sword. Then our battle began. I began to move so fast the ghoul could not see me, except for a fireball. I leaped into the air, coming down on him, knocking him to the ground. He begun to burn from my fire. I brought my sword down, severing his head. I looked down at the body. I should have been pleased, but something was wrong. The fire was trying to consume my very soul. The fire continued to build within me. I could not stop it. I felt as though I was going to explode! I screamed out in agony, as the fire consumed me. Camaz had managed to get up. He ran up to me but I scream out, "Stay back, my love! The fire is consuming me from within! I will not let it take your life along with mine!" I began to cry tears of fire saying, "I love you with all of my heart and soul, please do not morn me, my love, for know this, I will always love you even in death!" He screamed out, "No, I will not go on without you this time! If you must be consumed by the fire I shall be consumed with you!" He ran up to me, pulled me into his arms and his body bursts into flames as well. I tried to push him away, but he was to strong. He placed his hands on my face saying, "I will love you for all of eternity, for you are my love, my life, my everything!" He pulled me to his lips, kissing me with all within him. Then something strange began to happen, the fire began to subside. Slowly at first, but the deeper he kissed me, the quicker the fire left me and I felt my heart soar taking wings. I opened my eyes to no fire. I broke our kiss saying, "Wow, you have put out the fire in my soul! Thank you my love!" He smiled at me saying, "I could not let you go. I would have rather died than to go on without you again! You are my one true love. There can never be another!" I watched in horror as he went down. He was so weak from blood loss, I had to act quickly. I screamed out to Devil and Sonja, telling them to go find two evils for us. They took off like the wind. I bit into my wrist, letting my blood pour into his wounds. I watched as his wounds begin to seal. I pulled him into my lap, offering him my neck and said, "Drink, my love and come back to me." I felt him gently bite down and began to drink. About ten minutes later I began to feel the blood loss taking hold of me. But Devil and Sonja returned with our prey. My prey smelled of pure evil. Camaz released my neck and pulled his man to him, drinking him down. I had done the same with mine. I could feel my strength begin to return, but I was still very weak. So was Camaz. Devil picked me up into his arms, Stantos done the same with Camaz. They both took off running toward our compound. We arrived there about an hour later. We were taken down to our quarters and placed on our bed. Stantos told us he was going to the holding cells to bring us more to eat. Devil spoke, "My queen, you scared the shit out of me when you burst into flames! I have never seen anything like that in all of my life! Do not ever do that to me again!" I laughed and said, "Sure, no problem, just remember to never really piss me off!" We all busted out laughing. After we had finished our meals Stantos had brought us and everyone had left Camaz said, "My god, woman what the hell happened to you! You scared me to death. I could not bare to watch you burn to death in front of me!" "I'm not sure what happened.

All I know is when I watched the ghoul prepare to take your life, the hatred began to build in me, setting my soul and body on fire!" He pulled me to his chest, stroking my hair and said, "Oh, how I love you, my beautiful queen. I would die before I would go on with out you!" "As I love you! I think your love is what put out the fire. Remember what Cassandra said. Only you could save me. I think she knew what was going to happen. Your love and passion for me is what put the fire out. I felt it lessen as you began to kiss me." "I must remember to kiss you like that again if I ever piss you off!" We both burst out laughing, I said playfully, "Come here!" I pulled him to my lips, kissing him passionately. He pulled me on top of him. I broke out kiss, looking down into those beautiful green eyes and said, "Take me, my need is great!" He placed his hands around my waist, lifting me, bringing me down onto him. I screamed out as he entered me. I sat up straight, riding him ever so slowly. My passion was building so I began to ride harder and harder. I watched the pleasure increase on his face. Suddenly I was under him. I watched the passion ignite in his eyes. He began slow steady strokes, bringing me over and over. He pulled me up into his arms, sinking his fangs into my neck. I screamed out my pleasure over and over as he drank. It was my turn, I bit him, causing him to explode as I drank. We just sat there riding our extreme lovemaking to it's end. I withdrew from him, rolling onto my side of the bed. We laid there for a few more minutes, enjoying the aftershocks. He pulled me to him. I fell off blissfully to sleep in his arms. That night while I slept our god Cassandra came to me. She explained the fire was another of the gifts she had bestowed upon me. But, because I did not understand what was happening, I could not control it. That was why she warned me to keep Camaz close, only he could save me. She told me his love for me was what keep me from burning to a crisp. But now I knew how to control it and it would be one of my best weapons in the future. With that, she left me. I had no other dreams that night.

CHAPTER 44

THE TWINS COMING OF AGE

It had been six months since the war with the ghouls. We had rid

our lands of their pestilence. The twins would be turning three and

would become adults. We were currently making preparations for

their coming of age party. They had grown into fine young adults.

They look so much like their lost brother and sister, it is uncanny.

Camazotz had trained well and had became as mighty a warrior as

his father. Jade had grown into a stunning beauty, but was also as

skilled as her brother. When it came to the daggers, she out did

them all. She so reminded me of myself. Looking at them made

me yearn for my other children, lost during the hunter's attack. The

next evening was their coming of age party, so I was busy making

last minute arraignments. As I sat on our bed, going over

everything Camaz came over to me, sat down and placed his hand

on my face. I looked up at him smiling. God how the man made my heart sing! He asked, "My dear, are you ready to hunt? I am quite thirsty." "Yes, shall we go?" I got up, went to my closet and dressed in one of my hunting outfits. He came up to me, pulled me to him, hugging me to his chest and said, "My beautiful queen, oh how happy you make me. I thank our god every night for giving you back to me!" I raised my face to him, smiling. He kissed me tenderly. I broke our kiss, grabbed his hand, pulling, "Come, my love, let us hunt." We were deep in the heart of the city, sitting atop a building, looking down at the darken streets. I closed my eyes, letting my sense of smell take over. Soon I picked up on a scent. I smiled at him and said, "Dinner is served!" We leapt into the air, following the wonderful smell until we reached a small house on a dimly light street. From the scent, there were two evils inside. I searched for the blood of innocents inside, but could not smell any. I told Camaz I was in the mood for the game and landed in front of the house. I was in my leather bra and pants. I knew the evils inside were killers of many woman. As my husband had said, no man could resist my body. I walked up onto the porch and knocked. Soon a tall, handsome man answered the door. He asked me if he could help. I proceeded to tell him I was on my way to a party but my car had broken down and asked if I could use his phone to call for help. He invited me into the house and took me to the kitchen, where the phone was located. I pretended to call for help and asked if I could wait for the tow truck. The man answered, "Why sure pretty lady, have a seat, would you like something to drink?" "That would be nice, thank you." He went to the fridge and returned with a soda, handing it to me. I thanked him and took a sip. Suddenly another man walked into the kitchen. He was slightly shorter then the first man and not as handsome. He said, "Jorge, who is your friend?" Jorge proceeded to explain I had broke down and was waiting for the tow truck. I watched as the second man began to eye me up and down. I could see the lust began to build in his eyes. I smiled to myself, thinking, "Let the games begin!" I asked the men if I could use the restroom, I was told it was upstairs and they would show me the way. I followed the two men upstairs and into a bedroom. I asked, "Where is the bathroom? I do not see one in this room." The next thing I knew the tall man had grabbed me, slinging me onto the bed. The other man grabbed my hands, pulling them above my head. The tall man began to undress me, exposing my breast. He fondled them for a minute and began to pull my pants off. My blood lust was beginning to build within me. I called out to Camaz in my head, "I have tired of this game, let's eat." The tall man had me completely naked on the bed and was removing his pants when Camaz walked into the room. The man holding my arms yelled, "Who the hell are you!" I began to laugh and he asked me, "What is so funny?" I looked him in the eye and said, "Why this my husband, king of Mexico and he is going to kill both of you!" "He is not our king. I know what our king looks like!" I smiled at him, baring my fangs and said, "He is not your human king, he is Camazotz king of the vampires!" I watched as the horror of what I had told him reached his eyes. The man released me, yelling to the other man, "Run that is the devil himself!" They both took off running, trying to get out of the house. But we were just to fast for them. I leapt on the taller man, knocking him to the ground face first. Camaz had the other man down also. My prey was fighting me fiercely, trying to get me off of him. I rolled him over onto his back, pulling his arms above his head and struck. His sweet blood began to flow. As I slowly drained him I could feel his heart start to slow. I withdrew long enough to look him in the eye and said, "For all of the evil you have done, I claim your life as mine!" I stuck again, draining him the rest of the way. I stood up from his body and watched the light leave his eyes. Camaz had also finished his meal, so he grabbed my hand and said, "Come, my queen, let us go home!" We arrived back at the castle around 4am. We checked on the children and went to our quarters. I went to our bed to finish what I had been working on when we left to hunt. He came over smiling down at me and said, "Shall I draw us a bath, my love?" "That would be wonderful my love. I am almost finished here." He went to the bathroom to run our bath. I had finished the final planning for the twins party, so I got up, remove all of my clothing and went to my dressing table to brush my hair out. As I was brushing I heard him enter the room. He came up behind me, lifted me to my feet, turning me to face him. He was also naked. I stared at his beautiful body and my lust for him ignited way down low. He lifted me into his arms and carried me into the bathroom. He got into the tub, sitting with me in between his muscular legs. I laid my head back on his chest and whispered, "I love you. You are my heart, my life, my everything!" He grabbed the sponge and began to wash me. He knew how much I love that and how it excited me. He began to carcass my breasts. I lifted my face to him. he bent to my lips and began to kiss me ever so gently. He deepens the kiss as I reached up, wrapping my arms around his neck, bowing my chest out to him. I felt his manhood become rock hard up against my back, igniting my passion to the fullest. I grunted out my pleasure to him. He grabbed my hips, raising me to him without breaking our kiss and entered me. I screamed out my passion into his mouth. His slow steady stokes pushed me to the edge. I turned with him inside of me, facing him. I stared into his beautiful green eyes. He smiled, pushing me over the edge. I began to ride him hard, quicker and quicker, until I exploded screaming his name over and over. I went to his neck, kissing it ever so gentle and bit. He screamed out my name, telling me how much he loved me as he released himself deep within me. He bit me, causing me to lock down on him and release the strongest orgasm I had ever felt. I felt as though I was floating in my ecstasy and would never come down. He licked the blood from the bite, sealing it. I did the same on his neck. We just sat there rocking in each others arms. He lifted me from him, causing shivers of delight down my spine and rolled us to our sides. I stared into his eyes, all the way to his soul. he had the most beautiful soul of anyone on this earth. I still could not understand how the humans could paint him as such a monster.

If they only knew the goodness within this man and how he had

protected them for almost a thousand years, they would come to

love him, as I had. He asked, "What are you thinking about, my

queen?" "Just how beautiful your soul is, my love and how the

humans so misunderstand you." "It has always been this way.

They fear me from the legends the Mayan people have told. But I

prefer it that way, my love, so our people are not endangered by

the humans." "You have such a good heart, my king. This is why I

love you so!" He pulled me to him and said, "It is you, my queen

that has such a good heart. You are so loving and strong. I could

feel it in you the day I saw you standing on the street waiting for

your ride so many years ago. I knew from that moment you where

my soul mate and I had to have you!" With his words I fell off to

sleep with the biggest smile I had ever had on my face. The next

evening when we woke we began to dress for the twins party. I

knew how much he loved to see me in emerald green so I had

purchased a stunning strapless crushed velvet gown. As I pulled the dress on he came over and zipped the dress up. He kissed me on my neck, telling me how beautiful I looked. I turned to him, thanking him with a kiss. He was dressed in black slacks, a white collared shirt, opened at the neck. He had a thin leather tie at his neck with our crest on it. He wore the signet ring I had given him years back on his right pinkie. He was absolutely stunning. He made my heart soar. I took my crown from the box. It was the one with the emeralds and diamonds. I handed it to him and he placed it on top of my head. I handed him the matching necklace, he latched it around my neck and kissed me, "Do you have any idea how beautiful you look tonight my dear? I so love that color on you! You are my heart and I will love you for all of eternity!" I turned smiling up at him and said, "As I will love you, my king. Every time I look into your eyes my heart sings for you!" He pulled me to his lips, kissing me tenderly. After a few minutes I broke our kiss and said, "Come, my love and let us honor our children on their coming of age." We left our quarters heading upstairs to the great hall. There were many in attendance, including some old friends. Louisa and Marylou, my best friends, had returned for the party. They had been ruling their countries since the loss of their husbands in the war against the hunters. My heart cried out for their loss. I so wished that terrible time had never happened. Their loss was great, including their children. I went up to them, hugging both and went to greet our other guests. Bodgan had survived the attack along with his son, but had lost all others. They both were there for the party. I went to our good friend Bodgan, hugged him and welcomed him back to our home. He smiled at me and proclaimed, "Anne, you are as beautiful as the first day I met you! How are you my good friend?" "I am doing fine, a little sad at the children reaching adulthood so soon though." He smiled at me and said, "Do not be sad, just know your children have grown into fine young adults and are here with you!" "Thank you, Bodgan, you are a good and true friend!" I had seen another of my friends, so I excused myself. Camaz stayed behind to speak with Bodgan. I went over to the table where Devil and Sonja were seated and say hello. They looked so in love! I knew they where meant for each other. Sonja was heavy with their first child. I was so excited for them. I visited with them a few more minutes and returned to the throne. Camaz was already there awaiting me. We both took our seats and Camaz called the party to order. Camazotz and Jade stood before the council and were proclaimed adults and heirs to our throne. We had decided to rule for a while. The children wanted to go to college and off on their own for awhile. I was sad, but I had to let them go. After the coming of age ceremony we called the party to order, congratulating our children and the music began to play. Camaz reached for my hand, leading me out onto the dance floor for the first dance. As we spun around the dance floor I placed my head on his chest and sighed saying, "Oh, how I am going to miss our children, my love, my heart is breaking!" He reached for my face, pulling it up so he could look me in the eyes, "My queen, I to feel your pain, but we must let them go, they are adults now." "But Camaz, we have gone through so much loss already. I am not ready for them to leave me! I could still feel the pain in my heart when I stared at our children lifeless bodies and how my heart shattered that night! Then when the twins were born, they put my broken heart back together!" The tears were rolling down my face. He wiped them away and said, "How I hate to see you cry, but just remember they are safe from the hunters because of you, my mighty warrior queen!" I smiled, for he is right. A few minutes later the children came up, letting us know they were going hunting with their friends. We told them to go ahead and have fun. I watched as my children took off running into the beautiful summer night. We visited with our friends for about an hour then went down to our quarters to make ready for the hunt. I went to my closet, pulled out my black leather bodysuit. For I knew how much he loved it. I pulled it up onto my body and went to him to zip it. I loved when he done that. He did it ever so slowly and passionately. Once he reached my neck he kissed right above the zipper. I turned to him saying, "Do you have any idea how hot you make me when you do that, you set my soul on fire!"He smiled and said, "As do you, my queen!" We left our quarters, heading up to ready for the hunt. Devil was sworn to protect me, but had asked if he could stay behind that night. Sonja was close to giving birth. I told him he needed to and said, "Do not worry, my mighty Devil, I will have more than enough protection. Bodgan is hunting with us tonight and we are taking Achilles and BamBam as well. So you stay behind to take care of Sonja." He reached for my hand, kissing the back and said, "You have a good and true heart, my queen!" I smiled at him and we left. Bodgan was outside awaiting us. Camaz asked, "So, my dear, do you feel like running or flying tonight?" I smiled up at him and shouted, "Running!" We all took off into the beautiful night. The dogs were right by our side. We reached a clearing in the woods. I stopped and tested the air for prey. But I picked up something else. I knew the scent. My hatred begins to build within me. I turned to the men and yelled, "I have scented hunters in the area!" I watched in horror as a arrow stuck Bodgan in the chest. He went down screaming. Camaz quickly picked him up and leapt into the air with me right behind him. I whistled for the dogs to head back to the castle. I had so wanted to stay behind. My hatred for the hunters was still fresh in my heart. I did not understand how it was possible. We had went all over the world and eradicated them all! A few minutes later we arrived at the castle, taking Bodgan right to the healers. We were told the arrow was to close to his heart, he was dying. With each of my tears that fell, the anger in my heart grew stronger. I went over to our good friend, looking into his dying eyes and proclaimed, "I swear with all that is in me I will make them pay for your death my dear friend! I will not rest until we have destroyed them all again!" I kissed him on the cheek, watching as the life left his eyes. Camaz went over to his friend, raising his sword and proclaimed, "I swear, my dear friend, their deaths will be sever and with each I will honor you with the kill!" We then left our friend, heading for our quarters. Once inside we went to our gear and dressed. When we where attacked, I caught the scent and was able to track them very easily. The dogs were awaiting us outside. We took off running to our elite compound in Cristos. Along the way we ran into the children. We told them of Bodgan's death and to go back to the castle, but they refused stating they were adults and it is their duty to protect our lands as well. So they came with us, I feared for their safety, but they were right, they were adults and had been very well trained. We arrived at our compound and called a meeting with our elite squad. They all had gathered in the war room. Camaz stood and announced, "The hunters have returned to our lands and have killed our good friend King Bodgan. We have swore on his death bed we will not rest until we have rid our lands of the hunters. So, make ready for battle, my mighty elite squad!" They all raised their weapons in the air and cheered for their king. The chant "Death to the hunters" began to fill the room. Just then Devil walked into the war room. I went over to him and said, "Why are you here my mighty Devil? I have ask you to say with Sonja." He answered, "Sonja has given birth and they are all fine. It is my duty to protect you, my queen. Sonja is the one who reminded me of this, telling me to come." We all left the compound, heading off in the direction where we were attacked. Soon we arrived in the area. I stopped, testing the air for the hunters scent. I caught the scent and told Devil to keep the children close to him. I knew they were mighty warriors in their own right, but I still feared for their safety, as they had never dealt with hunters. He replied, "As you wish, my queen." We were close to their camp, so we leapt to the trees to take them by surprise. There was about fifty hunters below us in the camp. I pulled my crossbow around and load the arrows. Jade had done the same. We both fired at the same time, taking out eight of the hunters. Now their camp was in complete cayuse. The hunters were running around trying to get to their weapons. We loaded again, fired and took out eight more. We all leapt from the trees, going after the hunters. I dropped my crossbow to the ground, reached around and brought my sword forward. I went for the first hunter in my path. He had his sword drawn as well. We met and began to battle. As we fought I said, "How dare you enter the lands of Death's Deliverer! We will kill all of you!" I swung my sword, taking the hunter's head. The anger and hatred had built so much within me, I felt my soul catch fire, along with my body. I watched as the stunned hunters just stood there, staring at me in disbelief. I went for the two in front of me with my sword flaming. I took both of their heads. By the time we were done all of the hunters have been destroyed. But my soul was still on fire and I could not bring myself down. I screamed out for Camaz, knowing only he could put out the fire deep within me. He rushed over to me, pulled me into his arms, telling me everything was alright and everyone is safe. I felt his love pour over me, drowning the fire within me. He smiled and said, "There is those beautiful blue eyes that I so adore!" I smiled up at him and said, "Thank you, my love." We knew we have destroyed all of the hunters there, but we had to continue our search, knowing where there was some, more would follow. But we had to return to the compound, daylight was coming.

CHAPTER 21

HUNT FOR THE HUNTERS

It had been several months since the attack that killed our good friend Bodgan. We went out nightly in search of the scum. We had taken down many hunters. I could not for the life of me figure out where they were all coming from! If there was that many in our lands, how many more were around the world. We had sent out messages to all the kingdoms, to see if they were having the same problems as we were. We received word back all of them were having the same problems as us. One day we received some disturbing news. The leader of the hunters was a vampire! Her name was Rose. From the reports she had been attacked by a rouge vampire. He changed her and left her all alone. The hatred for our kind had been within her every since. From what we were told, she was very evil. She was never taught to kill only evils. So she fed upon innocents because there was no blood bond to stop her. But one thing to our advantage was she was very young in vampire years, much younger than me. We had sent out scouts to try and find Rose, but it had been to no avail. We had just received a report a group of hunters had attack not far from us. There was also rumors Rose was with them. We quickly dressed in our battle gear and headed out to where the vampire was reported to be. We arrived at the location about one hundred miles from the compound. There in a large field we saw a great battle going on. There was many hunters, as well as vampires, werewolves, fairies and demons. I scanned the area, looking for Rose, hoping to spot her. We all took off running to the scene to help the others. Once we reached them we began to fight as well. I was in battle with two of the hunters when I heard a voice from behind me saying, "Well, well, if it isn't the mighty Death's Deliverer!" I could not turn to face her or the hunters would get me. I swung taking the first hunter's head and swung around taking the other hunter's head. I spun around to face Rose and said, "Yes, that is what they call me and you are about to find out why!" "Then come for me Deliverer!" I ran toward her, readying to battle. Just as I reached her, she sidestepped me, causing me to miss. I slammed into a tree, splitting it in half. I turned to go after her again. She began to laugh saying, "You have to do better than that! I am much stronger and quicker than you. For you see, I drink from the innocent, making me much more than you can ever be!" She leapt at me, knocking me to the ground. She swung, hitting me so hard the darkness took me. I screamed out in my head for Camaz, but I could hear nothing. I knew I was not dead yet because I could still feel our bond. But I was in total darkness, alone. Suddenly I came to. I tried to get up, but I could not move. I was strapped to some kind of table. I looked around my surroundings, trying to figure out where I was. Rose then walked into my view and said, "It will do you no good to try and escape, the table you are on is reenforced with magic to hold a vampire and the walls prevent you from contacting your man. Let me tell you what is going to happen. We are going to expose you to the world for what you are, then destroy you for all of human kind to see. This will start the war I have so longed for. Our kind is out numbered by the humans, so they will destroy all of us in the end!" I said, "How can you do this to your own kind! You are vampire, it is your job to protect our kind!" "What? Like your kind protected me when I was taken! Well let me tell you a little something about the vampire you love so much, he is the one that made me!" I screamed out, "Never, Camaz would never do that to an innocent! You lie!!" "Have you never read the stories of Camazotz? He is the most evil demon ever placed on this earth! Your love for him has blinded you of the truth!" I screamed out at her, telling her I would never believe any of her lies. She smiled at me and said, "As you wish, but when he comes for you, ask him. I will allow him to enter here to save you but then he will be trapped here with you. You will both die together!" She left the room, leaving me with all she had told me. I closed my eyes and began to think. I knew Rose was lying to me. I had been with my one true love and never once had I seen him cruel to any innocent. He had always helped them. I began to struggle, trying to free myself from my bonds. But they were just to strong. About an hour later I heard a great commotion coming from outside of the room where I was being held. Suddenly the door splintered and my love entered the room. I screamed out to him to go, that the room was reenforced with magic. But it was to late, he could not get out. He ran over to me, trying to break my bonds, but it was of no use. I watched as Rose appeared in the doorway. I heard some kind of chant and Rose spoke, "Well, mighty Camazotz, it seams I have trapped you! Now you shall pay for what you have done to me!" I looked up at him and said, "This crazy vampire is trying to tell me it was you who attacked her and left her on her own. Tell me this is not so, my king!" I watched as the shame entered his eyes. I screamed out, "No, this cannot be! You are not evil! I know the good that is in your heart. Please do not break my heart. Please, please, tell me she is lying!" I watched my true love turn into the thing the legend was all about. He had the head of a bat, with many sharp teeth in his mouth. He had huge black wings, but his body was the same body I loved so well. I began to scream over and over, "No! This is not possible. Please tell me this is a nightmare! Please, please, wake me from this horrible nightmare!" He spoke to me, " I am sorry, my love, but this is what I am. I would have gladly given up my life for you not to see me this way." I watched as blood tears began to run down his face. He then turned to Rose and said, "I am Camazotz, your god and creator. Release her from her bonds, I command you!" I watched as Rose succumbed to his will, telling who was with her to release me. I felt the bonds fall away. I got up from the table and walked up to him. I placed my hand on his face and said, "I do not care what you are. All I know is you are my one true love and there can be no other!" He roared out his pleasure with what I had said. He turned to Rose and commanded, "Come to me!" She walked into the room and stood before her god. He reached for her, pulling her to his mouth and bit her head off, throwing her body to the ground. He turned to me, enveloping me in those huge wings, hugging me to him. He whispered in my ear, "As I love you, my queen. Come let us leave this place." I looked up at him, he had changed back into himself. I pulled him to my lips and said, "I love you, my king. I do not care what you are, for you are mine as I am yours!" He kissed me tenderly. We then left that terrible place. Knowing their leader had been destroyed, all the hunters went into hiding. But we would not rest until we had wiped them off the face of the earth! In A few hours later, we were back in our quarters. Camaz asked me, "How can you look upon me after seeing what my true form is? Do I not repulse you, my queen?" "No, never. All I know is when you where in your true form, I looked into your beautiful eyes and I saw the man that stole my heart!" He pulled me to him, hugging me to his chest, "Oh how you please me with your words, my love! You are the love of my life and there can be no other. I was so afraid you would leave me when you found out about me. I promise I will never take the blood of the innocent again, you have my word!" "I know your thirst for human blood is strong, my love. I know the stories of you. I do not want you to do this for me, I want you to do this for yourself. If you cannot resist, I will understand!" "You have such a good heart, my queen. I do not deserve to have such happiness!" He pulled me to his lips, kissing me passionately. I broke our kiss and said, "Show me again, my king. I want to see you in all your glory!" I watched as he changed into the creature of myth. I said, "My god, you are beautiful!" I pulled him to me and said, "I want you to make love to me in your true form." He engulfed me in those huge wings and carried me to the bed. He laid me down, unfolding his wings. He looked down at me and said, "In all of my years I have never made love in my true form, are you sure this is what you want, my queen?" I grunted out my passion, letting him know just how much I wanted it. He smiled down at me with all those razor sharp teeth. I could see the happiness in his eyes. I felt him enter me. I screamed out my passion over and over. He was trying to be gentle with me, but he is driving me crazy with need. I pulled that huge mouth to me and said, "I need you badly. I do not care, do not be gentle with me!" He began to stroke faster and faster. I so wanted him to bite me. But I didn't know if he could with all those teeth. But he had pushed me over the edge. I struck him in the neck, his sweet blood flowed into my mouth. That drove him into a frenzy. I felt as he bit into my neck. But I did not feel all of those teeth, only his fangs. I looked into his face, he had changed just enough that his mouth was human. I watched as the pleasure took him. He unfolded those huge wings, wrapping them around me, pulling me up to him. We rocked back and forth while he drank. I whispered to him, "I love you, my mighty Camazotz!" He released my neck and pulled me to his lips, kissing me tenderly. My heart was flying with the love I felt for him. I felt my climax coming. I broke our kiss and screamed, "Now my love, I am so close, send me over!" He quickened his stroke. My eyes roll back in my head and I screamed out as I exploded. I felt him let go deep within me. he unfolded those great wings from around me and I watched as he threw back his head, screaming out my name. Slowly he began to change back. He laid on me for a few minutes then rolled to his side, pulling me into his arms. I whispered to him, "Never be afraid to make love to me in your true form. I love you for who you are and will until the end of time!" From that night on he made love to me in his true form. A few days later as we were out hunting for more hunters we came upon a strange sight. A creature I have never seen. It was gaunt to the point of emaciation. It's skin was pulled tautly over it's bones. It's completion was ash gray. The creature had four arms with long razor sharp claws on the hands. It's face was of a demon with glowing red eyes and razor sharp teeth. I looked at Camaz and asked, "What the hell is that thing?!" He then replied, "My dear, that is the Wendigo. I have not seen him in over one hundred years." "You know this creature?" "Yes, he is a friend of mine, but he disappeared over one hundred years ago. Come we must go talk to him." We descended down to where the creature was at. I watched Camaz change into his true form, he raised his hand and called out, "My good friend Igos, it has been many years!" The beast then spoke, "Yes it has my friend Camazotz, who is the beautiful lady with you?" "This is my wife and Queen, Anne." Igos bowed to me and said, "It is a pleasure, Lady Anne!" I smiled at him and said, Welcome, mighty Igos, come let us go back to the castle." We then left for home. Along the way Igos told us he had been wondering the world for the last one hundred years looking for a mate. "But I have yet to find a human suitable for me. They all fear me when they look upon me in my true form." Camaz told him, "For many years I feared showing Anne my true self, fearing I would lose her. But recently I had to. But she did not run from me, she ran to me. She still loves me for what I am!" "Oh, how I wish I could find such happiness!" I smiled at him and said, "You will some day and when you do, your heart will sing for her!" When we arrived back at the castle, needless to say, there was a lot of shocked faces. Not just because of Igos but also because Camaz had not changed back to human form. I watched as Jade came up to her father, smelled and said, "Father, is that you?" "Yes, my child, it is I. This is your father's true form, do I frighten you?" "No father, not at all, you just took me by surprise." She hugged him to her. He warped his wings around her and said, "Oh, how happy you make me, my child. I love you with all that is within me!" She looked up at him, touched her hand to his face and said, "As I love you, Father!" Camazotz came into the room and said, "Welcome home, Father and Mother." I looked at him in amazement, how did he know that was his father! Then I was in total shock when Camazotz unfurled his wings. "You have wings! Just like your father!" "Yes Mother. I discovered them the night of my coming of age." I turned to our daughter and asked, "Do you have wings also?" "No, Mother, only the males do." Oh how that had sounded familiar. I thought back to my first meeting with our good friend Dempie when he told me only female fairies had wings. Later after we have introduced Igos to everyone we asked if he would like to stay with us. He replied, "I would love to but I must continue my search for my one true love. Lady Anne, you have sparked something deep within me with the hope I will find her." He said his goodbyes and was gone into the night We would see him many years later, but I am getting ahead of myself.

CHAPTER 22

THE BEAUTIFUL SUN

It had been one year since Igos left us. I so hoped he would find his one true love and could be as happy as we were. I had told Camaz I wanted to be in the sun very much, so he had made plans for us to go to the island. He stayed in his human form most of the time. But when we were alone he was always in his true form. But when I looked upon him all I could see was the man I feel in love with. But he told me when we are in the sun he would be in his human form because he couldn't go into the sun in his true form. I told him, "I do not care what form you are in, my love, as long as you are with me." He pulled me into his arms, wrapping those great wings around me and kissed me. I whispered into his mouth, "Not now, my love, I am starving!" He chuckled and transformed back into his human form. He grabbed my hand and said, "Let us go, I do not want my queen to miss a meal because of me!" I laughed at what he had said and we took off into the beautiful night. Soon we were deep in the woods, searching for prey. I stopped, testing the air. I soon picked up on a scent. I pointed off to the west. We then took off running. Suddenly I stopped. He stopped with me and asked, "What is wrong, my love?" "I just had a thought, I want you to hunt in your true form. I have never seen this and I love to watch you hunt." "As you wish, my queen." He transformed, taking me into his arms and began flapping his mighty wings. We were soon high above the forest. We spotted our prey. There was three of them down below. He dropped down onto a high tree, leaving me there. Then I watched as he took back to the air. He swooped down and landed in front of the men. I watched as the horror took them. They were all frozen with fear. I could smell it rolling off of them. Then they all took off running, screaming as they went. I watched Camaz leap on one of the men, knocking him to ground. God he was so beautiful. He bit down on the man's neck, severing his head from the body and lifted the body over his head, allowing the blood to pour into his mouth. Watching him do that had set my soul on fire with need. I dropped from the tree and went after the other two men. Their blood was calling to me, setting my throat ablaze. I could hear Camaz above me. I knew he was watching because like me, he loved to watch me hunt. I caught up with the two men and leaped at one, knocking him to the ground. He screamed out in terror. But when he saw it was me and not Camaz he began to fight me. Very stupid on his part. I slammed my fist into his face, shattering all of the bones. He screamed out in pain. The blood was pouring from the wounds, causing my killing instinct to take over. I slammed his head to the side, stuck and began to drain him. I heard the other man scream out. I looked up from my kill and watched Camaz tear the man apart. That ignited my passion. I cried out to him, "I desire you here and now, my king! My need is great!" He came over to me, pulling me up into his arms. I watched as all those razor sharp teeth disappeared. He then pulled me to his lips, kissing me deeply. I began tearing at my clothes, trying to get them off with out breaking our kiss. He whispered into my mouth, "Allow me, my queen." I felt the clothes rip from my body. He lifted me to him and as he entered me I screamed out my pleasure. He deepened the kiss, setting my soul on fire. I opened my eyes and looked into those beautiful green eyes. I saw past the beast. All I saw was my beloved. I felt my time was close so I broke our kiss saying, "My love, I am so close. Bring me over the cliff, make my heart take wings and soar!" He smiled at me and quickened his thrusts. I locked my legs around his waist and let my orgasm take me. I screamed out his name over and over with each thrust. Then I felt him explode deep inside of me. He wrapped his wings around me in a loving embrace. I laid my head on his chest and said, "I love you!" He leaped into the air, unfurled his wings and carried me back to the castle. When we arrived home he landed just outside of the entrance, wrapped his wings around my naked body and carried me down to our quarters. He unfurled his wings, setting me down in front of him. I watched as he changed back into his human form. God, he was so beautiful in both forms, it made my heart ache. We went to our bed and made ready for sleep. He pulled me to his chest and said, "My god woman, you are amazing! I cannot believe you love me for what I am. You complete me in all ways!" I looked up at him and said, "I do not care what form you are in, all I see is the man inside, the man I fell in love with!" He stoked my face saying, "You are my heart and there can be no other!" With that I fell off to sleep with a big smile on my face. The next evening we left for our island. We arrived about an hour later and made ready to walk in the sun. I knew I could not have him in his true form, but I did not care as long as he is with me. We walked onto the beach hand in hand. The sun began to rise. I felt it's wonderful warmth on my face. I smiled my pleasure and I felt the tingle on my skin, letting me know the change was coming. I turned toward Camaz and smiled. He smiled back at me as our bodies changed to a pale glowing red. Camaz stated, "My god woman, I still cannot get over how stunning you are in the sunlight!" His words made my heart soar. We laid down on the beach and enjoyed the sun for hours. He rolled to his side, staring down at me and said, "Are you happy, my queen?" "Yes, my love, you make me very happy!" He pulled me to him and kissed me. I could feel my passion growing. I grunted out, letting him know I needed him. He smiled and said, "My love, do you prefer my human form here or my true form inside of the house?" "My need is great. I do not know if I can wait till we are in the house!" He pulled me on top of him and slowly began to kiss me. Then he intensified the kiss. The man was driving me crazy with need! I raised up from him and positioned myself over his manhood. Then I slowly lowered myself. He reached up to caress my breasts. I started a slow steady rhythm. I stared into his eyes and watched as the lust began to take him. He sat up and began to thrust, meeting me as I came down. I threw my head back, screaming up at the sun. Between the sun and him they had set my soul on fire. I screamed over and over as the orgasm rocked me. I felt him let go. I dropped my mouth to his neck and bit, he then bit me. We rocked back and forth as we savored each others blood. Afterward he pulled me to his lips. I could taste both of our blood as it intermingled in our mouths. After a few minutes of kissing I rolled off of him and enjoyed what was left of the sunlight. Dusk would be upon us soon and we would go to the mainland to hunt. We had brought our battle gear with us because there was still the threat of the hunters. The hunters had gone underground, so we did not know how many were left. I put on my black leather bodysuit and placed all of my weapons. We went out into the beautiful night. I watched as he changed forms. Then he took me into his arms, leaped, spread his wings and flew us to the mainland. I put my head on his chest and said, "I love you, my mighty Camazotz!" "As I love you, my queen!" We sat atop a tall building in town, looking down on the city. I scented the air looking for prey. suddenly I caught a scent not far from us. I leaped to the ground and began to stalk my prey. Camaz was above me. I saw two men off in the distance, standing on a street corner. The smell coming off of them was driving me crazy, but I was in the mood for a game. I looked up at Camaz and smiled. I heard him say in my head, "Does my queen wish to play with her food first?" "Oh how I do!" I heard him chuckle. I started walking toward the men. I watched their eyes as I approached. I could see the lust in them. I stopped in front of them and said, "Hello, I seem to have lost my pet, can you gentlemen help me?" I heard Camaz roar with laughter at what I had said. One of the men asked, "Sure, what does he look like?" "He is beautiful, with long black hair and emerald green eyes." The other man said, "Let's go back to my house and we will get the car so we can look for your dog." I looked at the men oddly and said, "Dog, what dog?" The first man asked, "You didn't lose a dog?" "Why no silly, my pet has great black wings and a mouth full of very sharp teeth!" I then looked up to the sky and proclaimed, "Oh there he is!" Camaz sat down beside of me. I watched as the horror built in their eyes. They took off running. I said to Camaz, "Me first!" I took off running after the men. I knocked one of them to the ground. He screamed out in terror and tried to knock me off. I heard the other man scream out as Camaz took him down. I turned my man over. He looked up at me and I smiled, baring my fangs. He said, "What the hell are you and what is that thing with you?" "I am a vampire silly and that is my husband, the mighty Camazotz!" I slammed his head to the side and struck, drinking him down. Oh how sweet his blood was! I watched my love lift the headless body above him and let the blood pour into his beautiful mouth. He tossed the body to the side, walked up to me, taking me into his arms. We flew into the night sky, heading back to our island. We had been on the island for two weeks. I was missing our family, so I was ready to go back home. But not before I walked in the sun one more time. As the sun began to set I sighed. Camaz asked me, "What is wrong, love?" "I am going to miss this so much!" "We can stay longer if you would like." "No, I am ready to go home. I miss the children." "Very well. I will go pack everything and we shall go." A few hours later we were back home. The children came up hugged us and welcomed us home. Jade said, "Oh how I have missed you Mother and Father! It has been so lonely here without you!" "We have missed you as well, my daughter!" I went over and hugged Caamzotz. He smiled and said, Welcome home Mother, I have missed you so much!" Oh how those children were my heart. I closed my eyes and thanked our god Cassandra for giving them back to us. Just then Devil came into the room. he told us Astor needed to speak with us. We headed toward the Council's chambers. We said our hellos to Astor and sat down to speak. He told us he had just received word an encampment of hunters had been located about fifty miles from us. We told him to get word to our Elite of what was going on and we would be there the following evening. We left and met with Devil, to let him know what was going on. Once we were inside of our quarters I said, "My love, will we never be rid of the vermin. My hatred is already building in my heart. I just want to go now and tear them all to pieces!" He pulled me into his arms and wrapped his wings around me saying, "I know how you feel, my queen, but daylight is approaching quickly. We would not make it there in time. We will wait until tomorrow evening." He raised my face to him, kissing me tenderly. I smiled up at him and said, "My king, I am in need of a bath, would you like to join me?" I watched as he changed back into his human form. He picked me up, caring me into the bathroom. He sat me down on the chair and went to the tub to start the water. I stood up, removing all of my weapons. He came over to me, turned me around and slowly begun to unzip my bodysuit. Oh how I loved when he undressed me! He turned me around to face him. I smiled up at him. He pulled the suit from my arms, exposing my breasts. He pulled it all the way down, removing the suit completely. I stood in front of him in my nakedness. He smiled and said, "My queen, you have the body of a goddess! Oh how I crave your body!" I placed my hand on his face, smiled and said, "Boy you sure know how to get what you want, don't you, my king!" He pulled me to his lips, kissing me passionately. He lifted me up, caring me to the tub and got in without breaking our kiss. I could feel the heat began to build way down low. I moaned my pleasure into his mouth. He broke our kiss, smiled that I hunger for you my queen smile. He stood up from the tub with me in his arms, carried me to the bed and laid me down. I looked up at him and said, "Change for me, my king!" I watched as those great wings unfurled as he changed. He hovered over me, smiling down at me saying, "Are you ready for me, my queen?" I pulled him down to me, showing just how much I was ready! I felt him enter me, sending me over the edge. I began to scream over and over as he thrust in and out of me. I felt my release coming, so I bit into his neck, letting him know I was ready. He quickened his strokes, sending me over the edge and he bit me. I felt him explode inside of me. I began to lick his neck, savoring his blood. I was floating in my pleasure. That night I dreamed, I saw all of our lost children and friends. They all looked so happy. Then I was standing before our god. She said, "It is good to see you again, my child. I hope you are happy." "Yes, I am very happy, thank you for giving us back the children!" "You are very welcome, my champion. But I have brought you here to tell you a great battle is coming. The hunters are joining forces with the ghouls. Your entire kingdom is in danger from the attack. Please guard your children well, for they will try to take them from you." With that I wake up shivering. The tears were flowing down my face, I felt him wipe them away asking, "What is wrong, my love, have you had a bad dream?" "No it was a good dream, I saw all of our lost children and family but afterward I saw Cassandra, she has told me a great battle is coming and the hunters have joined forces with the ghouls. They are going to try and take our children from us!" "Never! I promise I will let no harm come to our children. I will protect them with my life, as I will you also. I am Camazotz, god of darkness. They have no idea who they are dealing with!" I smiled up at him and said, "My mighty warrior I know you will, as will I." We got dressed and went up to warn everyone about what was coming. We had Devil round up everyone and we headed to our elite squad's headquarters. We had brought Jade and Camazotz with us for save keeping. They would be very well guarded in the compound. Stantos was waiting when we arrived. He informed us all had been made ready. We tried to have the children go down below, but they refused to leave our side. They were grown, so we couldn't force them to stay below while we put our lives on the line. The children were very skilled fighters but I told Camaz we needed to keep them close to us. Just then, one of our scouts came into the room, announcing he have located the lair of the hunters and ghouls. We quickly dressed for battle and headed out. The location was about one hundred miles from our compound. We quickly arrived there. The children were right by us. We looked down upon the hunter's encampment. There was thousands down there! I felt the hatred begin to build within me. How dare they enter our lands and threaten my children! I pulled my sword from my back and made ready to attack. Camaz had

changed into his true form and roared out his anger. I watched as

the hunters stood there in disbelief. Then I heard one scream out,

"That is Camazotz, god of death, run for your life!" We watched

them scatter like the rats they were, but the ghouls showed no fear.

We watched as they drew their weapons and their leader screamed

out to the hunters, "Come back, you cowards! They cannot defeat

us all, even if they have the demon god with them!" We watched

the hunters turn, returning to the sides of the ghouls. I heard the

ghoul's leader bark out the order to attack. The next thing we were

battling for our lives. I watched as our son took on a hunter. He had

the man beheaded within seconds. I looked around for Jade. I

spotted her on the ground with two ghouls on her. I screamed out,

"No!" I felt the fire ignite within me, burning me to the core. I burst

into flames, but I knew how to control the fire. I pulled my sword

in front of me. It bursts into flames. I ran toward my daughter and

leapt, knocking both ghouls off of her. I brought my flaming sword down into one of the ghoul's chest, setting the beast on fire. I quickly took after the other, taking him out as well. I pulled into myself, felt Camaz's lips upon mine, killing the fire. I reached for Jade, helping her to her feet. She smiled and said, "Mother, you are amazing!" "Thank you, my child, let us go, we need to help the others." We ran off in the direction were I had left Camaz and Camazotz. I spotted Camaz, he had a hunter high above his head. I watched as he ripped the man in half. He flung the two halves to the ground. I looked for Camazotz. He was in battle with a ghoul. The ghoul ran at Camazotz, swinging his sword. I watched as Camazotz unfurled his wings and took to the air, making the ghoul miss him. He swooped down, swung and took the ghoul's head. He landed beside of us and we took off after a group of hunters. As we reached the hunters I watched in horror as one pulled the bow back and let his arrow fly, it was aimed at Camaz. I screamed out in horror, leaping in front of him. I felt the arrow strike me in the chest. I fell to the the ground screaming as the silver began to burn.

I heard Camaz roar out, screaming, "No, No, No! Please this cannot be!" He grabbed me up into his arms, leaping into the sky. I looked up at him, watching the tears roll down his face. I whispered, "My love, you must go back, you need to protect our children! Remember Cassandra's warning. I am dying my love, there is nothing you can do for me." He screamed out in pain and landed in a field, lying me down on the soft grass. "I promise I will be back, my love, I will not let you die alone!" He leaped into the sky and was gone. I stared up at the beautiful night sky. I was going to miss the sight of it. I began to cry as pain began to take me. I felt the darkness calling me. I screamed out, "No, do not take me now, please, please, let me look upon my true loves face one more time!" My heart began to blaze, the silver was burning badly. I screamed out in pain over and over. Suddenly I began to slip into the darkness. But right before it took me I heard the sweet voice of my beloved. He was crying for me. I opened eyes and asked, "Are the children safe, my love?" "Yes, they are here with you." I looked up at my beautiful children. My heart was breaking. I did not want to leave them! But the darkness was taking me. I screamed out for Camaz. He pulled me up into his arms, stroking my face and said, "I am here, my love, do not cry. Know this, I will love you for all of eternity, for you are my heart. No one has ever loved me the way you have and there shall be no other!" He pulled me to his lips, kissing me tenderly. I felt his tears strike my face. Suddenly I heard our god's voice, saying, "Remember what you have within you child, fight! Release the fire!" With her words I felt the fire in my heart change. It turned into a blazing inferno. I screamed out to Camaz and the children to get back. He laid me down on the grass and stepped back. My body burst into flames, ten times hotter than ever before. I felt the arrow begin to soften. I reached to my chest, grabbed the arrow, pulling it out. I screamed out in pain as the arrow came out. After removing it I tried to bring the fire back into me, but it was to hot. I could not stop it. I screamed out to him, "Camaz, please, please, I am burning alive. I cannot put the fire out!" I felt him pull me up into his arms and his lips touch mine.

Slowly he began to kiss me. I felt my heart begin to cool along with

my body. I placed my hand on his face, stroking gently. I felt my

heart take wings and fly. I opened my eyes, staring into his

beautiful emerald green eyes. His face was streaked with blood

tears. I broke our kiss and said, "You have saved me, my one true

love. You have made my heart sing once again with the joy of

being with you!" He lifted me into his arms and took to the air,

carrying me back to the compound. The arrow had done great

damage, so I was still very weak. Once we were in our quarters he

laid me down on the bed, checking the wound. He told me the fire

had sealed the wound, but there would be a scar because his blood

could not heal a closed wound. I told him it didn't matter to me. He

said, "They have scared this beautiful body. I will not rest until they

have all paid with their lives!" He bent down, saying, "Drink, my

love, come back to me in all of your glory!" I bit down, feeling his

sweet blood begin to flow. His healing blood brought my soul alive and made my heart heal from the inside out. I was still very weak and it would take me months to recover from the damage the arrow caused to my heart. But I knew Camaz would be by my side. About a month after the attack that almost ended my life for the second time, I was laying in our bed. I was still very weak from the damage the arrow had inflicted. Camaz had stayed by my side the whole time. He had our food brought in. The children were there visiting me. Jade was sitting on the edge of the bed, holding my hand and said, "Oh, Mother, I have missed not having you with me during the hunt. It is just not the same." I smiled up at her saying, "I know, my child. I to miss the hunt! I so long to run through the woods again. To feel the wind on my face!" Camazotz came over to me, smiled and said, "It is so good to see you getting better Mother. That night my heart broke when I though we were going to lose you!" I reached up, touching his face and said, "You are a good son! I am so proud of you. You fought bravely that day. You so remind me of your Father." Camazotz smiled down at me. I could see the pride in his eyes from my words. I tried to sit up, but the pain in my heart stopped me. I dropped back down onto the pillow. Camaz told the children I needed my rest, so they kissed me goodbye and left the room. Camaz came over to me, lifted me into his arms and said, "I am so sorry I did not protect you, my love, you should have let the arrow take me!" I pulled his face to me saying, "Never, never, say that again! You are my whole life. I would gladly lay my life down for you again and again if it meant keeping you safe!" "I do not deserve such a wonderful woman! I thank Cassandra every night before my sleep for bringing you back to me! You are my one true love and there can never, ever, be another!" He pulled me to his lips, kissing me tenderly. He broke the kiss and said, "Drink, my love and get well for me." I went to his neck, bit down, taking in his life giving blood. Oh how sweet his blood was. Just then there was a knock at the door. I released Camaz's neck and he laid me back down on the bed. He then told Astor to come in. Astor came in and asked, "How are you this evening, my queen?" "I am feeling a little better, thank you for asking." He then told Camaz our dinner was out in the other room. Once Astor left, Camaz brought me my meal and said, "Drink, my love, build your strength, so you can come back to me in all your glory." I pulled my meal to me and struck. His blood was so evilly sweet! I drink him down quickly. Camaz removed the body from the room and came back over to the bed. He pulled me into his arms, telling me how much he loved me. He raised my face to him, bent and kissed me ever so gently. I fell off to sleep in his arms. The next evening when I woke, I told Camaz I would like to get up for a bit. I wanted to enjoy the night sky. He picked me up from the bed and carried me out to the gardens. He placed me on the bench. I looked up at the night sky and sighed, "Oh, how I have missed this beautiful sight! How I long to run again my love!" "Soon my love you will regain your strength and you will be able to run like the wind!" I looked up at him, smiled and said, "Change for me, my king, I have missed your true form." He changed, unfurled his wings, warping them around me. I felt my heart soar with the love I felt for him. He was so beautiful to me, in ether form. I still couldn't believe he was mine for all of eternity. I watched as just his face changed back to human form. He pulled me to his lips, kissing me. I broke our kiss and said, "I want to fly, my love. I want to feel the wind on my face." He picked me up into his arms and leaped into the air and his mighty wings began to flap. Soon we were soaring in the sky. Oh how I had longed for this since my attack. The tears began to fall down my face, he asked, "What is wrong, my beloved? Why do you cry?" I answered "These are tears of joy, my love. Oh how happy you have made me. I have longed to feel the wind on my face, thank you!" A few minutes later he sat down in a field of beautiful flowers, the smell was overwhelming. he laid me down on the soft grass and I looked up at the beautiful night sky. The moon was full and the stars were shining brightly. He hovered over me with those great wings out spread and said, "I am so happy I have pleased you, my queen. I would do anything to make you happy." I smiled up at him and asked playfully, "Anything?" "My queen, you are still very weak. I would not want to hurt you!" "But I burn for you, my love. It has been to long, my need is great!" He stoked my face and said, "As you wish. But you must tell me if I am hurting you." He began to undress me. I could feel my fire for him ignite deep down. He stood, changing back into his human form. He did not want to take the chance of hurting me in his true form. He hovered over me. I pulled him down to my lips, kissing him passionately. I felt him enters me, sending me into a frenzy. It had been to long. I howled out my delight. He was going slow and steady, trying not to hunt me. But he was pushing me over the edge. I rolled him over so I was on top. I began to ride him. I sat straight up, throwing my head back, screaming out my pleasure. He reached for my breast and began to stroke them. Suddenly I felt him run his hand over the scar at my heart. I knew how much it pained him to have me marked in that way. I lowered myself back down to him, meeting his lips. I was so close, I could feel it coming. I locked myself around him as I released my orgasm, causing him to scream out his pleasure. He then exploded within me. We just laid there, enjoying each other. I smile at him and said, "Thank you, my love, you have made my heart soar with happiness." He kissed me tenderly. A few minutes later we got dressed. He asked, "Are you ready to go back home, beloved?" I smiled and answered, "Yes, but I feel like running!" I took off in a sprint. He quickly caught up with me. I was so happy, the pain in my heart began to subside. Then it took wings and flied. I stopped dead in my tracks. Camaz asked, "What is wrong, my love, has it been to soon for you to run?" "Oh, no, my love, the happiness of our lovemaking and the run has chased the pain away. My heart is flying right now!" He took me into his arms, swung me around and around and said, "Welcome back, my mighty warrior queen!" He spun me faster and faster. I was laughing the whole time. He set me down, "You have made me the happiest man on earth. Oh how I love you!" A few minutes later we took off running back to the palace.

CHAPTER 23

THE WINDIGO RETURNS

It had been two years since the terrible attack and I had fully recovered. We were out hunting when we come upon a familiar scent. It was our friend, Igos. We headed off in the direction the scent was coming from. There, in a open field we spot him. He was not alone. There was a young woman with him. We went to the field and greeted him. Camaz had not changed. He did not want to frighten the woman. We greeted our friend and welcomed him back. He then introduced the woman, "My good friends, this is my true love, Alissa. We are soul mates and she has agreed to become my bride." I could see the joy in Igos's eyes. I went up to the girl and said, "Welcome Alissa. I am Queen Anne and this is my King, Camaz. We are very pleased to meet you!" She smiled at us saying, "The pleasure is mine, your Highness." We all headed back to the castle. Once home we introduce her to everyone. I had

Maria go and make a room ready for our guests. I asked them when the wedding was to be. Igos replied, "We want to wed as soon as possible. That is why we have come here. We would like to ask your permission to wed here at the castle." I thought to myself, "Oh, goodie, a wedding! I must start the planning." I looked at Camaz, smiling. He stated, "I know that look, my queen. I take it the planning will begin now!" I laughed and answered, "Oh, how you know me so well, my king." We left the men to talk and I took Alissa down to my quarters. We started going over the wedding plans. While we were talking, she asked, " Igos has told me the story of you and the king. That once you where human, like me. Were you not frightened of the change?" "I was scared to death. But Camaz was with me the whole time, telling how much he loved me and how it would be over soon. When you find your one true love, you will do anything for him, including dieing. For my child, I have done just that. But our love is eternal and that is what brought me back to him from death." She smiled and said,

"I hope our love will be as strong as yours, Lady Anne!" We began the planning for their wedding. I summoned Maria and told her she needed to start on Alissa's wedding dress. I said goodnight to my new friend and went off to find Camaz. I found him and Igos in the Library talking. I let them know Alissa had retired to her quarters upstairs. Igos said his goodnight and went off to be with his true love. Camaz asked, "Are you ready for bed, my love?" I answered, "No, not right now. I would like to go for a walk in the gardens." He took my hand, leading me out to the gardens. I looked up at the beautiful night sky and proclaimed, "Beautiful!" He pulled me into his arms and said, "Not as beautiful as you, my queen. I have a surprise for you." He lead me into another part of the garden. Suddenly the smell hit me and I saw the blood red flowers everywhere. I cried out, "Oh, my, god. It is nightshade, thank you, my love. I have longed to smell them again." We walked amongst the nightshade, enjoying the wonderful smell and ourselves. I smiled up at him and said, "Oh my love you have made me so happy. You make my heart sing for you!" He pulled me back into his arms, kissing me with all the passion within him. He picked me up, caring me back to our quarters, never breaking the kiss. He laid me down on the bed and began to remove my clothing. I felt my heat ignite between my legs. He was driving me crazy. I watched as he removed his clothes. God his body was so beautiful. I cried out, "Show me, my king!" I watched him change for me, unfurling his wings. He came to the bed ,crawling up to me with those huge wings spread wide. God he was beautiful. As he hovered over me, he smiled. I could see the lust for me building in those beautiful green eyes. I reached for him, pulling him down to me. I watched as he changed his mouth back to human and he began to kiss me. He went to my neck, slowly kissing down to the base and licked all the way back up. That really pushed me over the edge and I screamed out, "Now, my love, take me now!!" I felt as he entered me. I screamed out his name and began to thrust my hips, meeting his every stroke. He pulled me up to his chest as I rode him. I looked into his eyes, smiled said, "You complete me in all ways! God how I love you! You are mine and I am yours!" With my words he quickened his strokes. I was so close I could feel it on my tongue. I threw back my head, screaming his name as the orgasm took me. He held me back and I watched as his wings unfurled with his pleasure. He was close, so I brought myself back up and began to ride him like a wild stallion. He grabbed my waist and I felt him thrust deep within me, letting himself go. I screamed out over and over with the pleasure he was giving me. Then something strange happened. I felt something release from my back. I heard him gasp and say, "My god, you have wings! Beautiful black wings!" I turned my head, looking behind me. I couldn't believe it, there they were! I began to cry with joy. He hugged me to him saying, "My god woman, you are becoming like me. Now the hunters will fear you even more. For they will know the true meaning of Death's Deliverer!" I cried out my joy with his words. I got up, going over to the mirror. I looked at my wings, they were so beautiful! I asked, "How do I conceal them, my love, as you do?" He answered, "All you have to do is pull them back into yourself with you mind, my love." So I tried it and they were gone. I ran to him, leapt into his arms, unfurled my wings again and wrapped them around him lovingly. The next evening I was so excited. I could hardly wait to try out my wings! I pulled at him saying, "Come, my king, let us fly into the beautiful night sky!" He chuckled and answered, "As you wish, my queen." We were outside and I looked up into the night sky, screaming my joy as my wings unfurled. I leapt into the sky. I felt the joy as my wings began to carry me though the sky. I was laughing so much I almost crashed into a tree. But he caught me just in time, pulling me away from the tree. We spun in midair with our joy and took off toward town. We landed on a building and I pulled my wings back in for I knew I could not hunt on the street with them out. I would scare the hell out of my prey. I tested the air for the unmistakable scent of pure evil and caught it. I leaped to the ground, stalking the scent. Camaz was high above me, as he loved to watch me hunt. I spotted my prey. He was standing near a alleyway. I began to play the game. I walked slowly toward the man, looking around as if I was lost. When I reached him I said, "Hello, I seem to have lost my way. I am looking for my friend's house, can you help me?" I smiled up at him. I could see the lust building in his eyes. He said, "Sure, my car is just down there. Come and I will take you to where you need to go." He had pointed to the alley. I smiled to myself and said, "Thank you, you are very kind." I followed him into the alley. I could sense Camaz sitting atop the ledge above us, watching. After we had gone a few feet into the alley I said, "I thought your car was in here." Suddenly the man jumped at me, knocking me into the wall. I started to scream, but he put his hand over my mouth saying, "If you scream, I will kill you. Now we are going to have some fun!" So I let him think he was overpowering me. He began to undress me until he had me naked. He stated, "My god, you are beautiful! You have the body of a goddess. I am going to enjoy you so much!" I looked him in the eye saying, "But you have not seen all of me yet!" I heard Camaz laugh in my head. The man asked, "What are you talking about, you are completely naked!" "But you have not seen my back. I have something very special on there." He spun me around, saying, "I see nothing on you back woman, stop playing with me." "Very well." I unfurled my wings, spreading them out for him to see. He began screaming, "What the hell are you?" "I am the thing of nightmares. I am mate to the mighty god, Camazotz!" He took off running. I took off after him, grabbed him and took to the air. Camaz joined me saying, "That was quite fun watching my love, so what is the plan?" "You will see, my love." All the time the man was struggling to get away from me. I yelled at him, "It will do you no good to fight me. I am 100 times stronger than you!" We were now over the woods. Camaz had picked up on his prey. He told me he would be right back and to have fun. I dropped down into an open area and released the man saying, "I will give you a five minute head start, then I am going to hunt you down like the animal you are! Now run for your life!!" The man took off running into the woods. A few minutes later Camaz sat down beside me and pulled me into his arms. I asked, "Did you enjoy your meal, my love?" "Oh yes, she was quite evil." "Well his five minutes are up and I am quite hungry, shall we?" We took off running in the direction the man has ran. We caught up with the him in seconds. I leapt at him, knocking him to the ground. He was screaming at the top of his lungs. I smacked him hard saying, "Shut up and hold still. I am starving!" I sank my fangs into his neck and began to drink. I listened as his heart began to slow and then stopped. I stood up from my kill, went over to Camaz. He took me into his arms saying, "You are amazing. Oh how I love to watch you hunt and feed!" We took to the air, flying back to the castle. The next evening I was with Alissa for her final fitting before the wedding. The gown Maria had created for her was beautiful. While I watched them working I thought back to Camaz and my wedding day and the beautiful gown Maria had created for me. Our fifty anniversary was coming up soon and I suddenly had a thought. I would talk to Camaz about renewing our wedding vows. But the focus was on Igos and Alissa's wedding. Their wedding was in three days and I still had so much to do. I headed down to our quarters to work more on the planning. He was there awaiting me. He pulled me into his arms, kissing me tenderly and asked, "Are you hungry, my dear?" "Yes, my love, but I would like to dine in tonight. I still have so much to do before the wedding." "As you wish, my queen. I will go down to the holding cells and bring our dinner up in a few minutes." He kissed me one last time and left the room. I went over to my desk to the computer, logged in and went to the site were I was ordering the flowers. Oh how I loved this modern age. I was able to order everything online and have it delivered in town at one of our werewolf friend's house. Then he would bring it here. It was now the night of the wedding. We were getting dressed. I had chosen a pale blue silk gown. I went to him

to zip up the dress. He slowly lifted the zipper. The whole time he

was kissing my neck. God, how the man excited me. He knew how

to push all the right buttons! I turned to him and said, "God, do

you have any idea what you do to me. You excite me in all ways,

my king!" He smiled and answered, "As do you, my love." I asked

him to go to my closet and retrieve my jewelery box. He brought it

back to me. I took my crown of blue and white diamonds out, hand

it to him, and he placed it upon my head. He took my necklace and

placed it around my neck. The large teardrop blue diamond rested

at the base of my throat. He pulled me to my feet saying, "I love

this color on you almost as much as emerald green. It so brings out

those big beautiful blue eyes!" I smiled up at him, thanking him.

He was dressed in black slacks a pale gray shirt and black vest. He

had his hair pulled back with a leather tie. His crown sat atop his

head. He was absolutely, stunningly handsome. Just looking at him

made my heart sing with joy. He took my hand and lead me

upstairs. We took our seats on the throne and the ceremony began. Igos was in human form and was very handsome. I watched his eyes sparkle when he saw his bride enter the room. She slowly walked down the isle until she reached him. He took her hand and they turned toward Astor. They said their vows, promising to love each other for all of eternity. Astor pronounced them wed and few minutes later we were all in the great hall for their reception. Igos took his bride out onto the dance floor for their first dance together. Camaz stood, reaching for my hand. He lead me to the dance floor. After we had joined the bride and groom, everyone else begins to dance. He held me close in those powerful arms. I placed my head on his chest and sighed. He raised my face and asked, "Are you happy, my queen?" "I am always happy, as long as I am in your arms, my love!" He smiled and bent for a kiss. After the dance we returned to our table and watched the happy couple. Igos would be taking her off to his home, later that night to change her from mortal, to immortal. Jade was sitting with us.

Camazotz was off with his friends. I watched a very handsome vampire come up to our table and asked Jade if she would like to dance. She accepted and they went to the dance floor. A few hours later we said goodbye to our friends and wished them great happiness. We went to our quarters to dress for the hunt. I removed all of my jewelery and handed the box to Camaz to put back in my closet. I had him unzip my dress and I stepped out of it, going to my closet to chose my hunting outfit. I put my leather pants on and took out my lace up leather top. He came up behind me and began to tighten the laces. He lifted my hair from my neck, kissing it. I laid my head back onto his chest and said, "You have such a good and gentle heart my love. I cannot understand why you are portrayed as such a monster." "My dear, before I met you my lust for human blood was unquenchable. I did not care if they were innocent or evil. But from the moment I met you my heart thawed. I swore on that day I would never take the blood of the innocent again. I have only slipped once, with Rose." "As I told you the night you showed your true self, I understand your thrust for human blood and if you slip every now and then, I understand." He hugged me to him and said, "You have such a good heart, my queen. I do not deserve such happiness!" After a few minutes we left for the hunt. Once we were outside he asked, "Shall we run or fly tonight, my love?" "Run!" I took off like a bat out of hell, with him right behind me. I yelled out, "Catch me if you can!" Then really turn on the speed. the next thing I knew I was on the ground, laughing my ass off. He looked down at me and I said, "I know, clumsiest vampire on earth." He busted out laughing, I reached for him, pulling him down on top me. Then our lips met. He wasn't laughing anymore. A few minutes later we were up running again. I stopped, testing the air. I picked up the scent of evil not far from where we were. I unfurled my wings and leaped into the air. Camaz was right behind me. Soon we came upon a campsite. There was four evils below, but there was also two innocents, a woman and child. They were both tied up in one of the tents. We landed on a tree, right above their camp and listened to them. They had planned on raping and murdering their hostages. I felt my blood begin to boil. Just as I began to leap to the ground I caught the scent of hunters. We watched as the hunters entered the camp. There were four men and three women. They introduced themselves to our prey and explained what they were looking for. The men burst into laughter and one of them asked, "Are you crazy? There is no such thing as vampires!" One of the hunters answered, "Just remember, we have warned you. They are out here somewhere and will find you!" Then the hunters left the camp. I said to Camaz, "We cannot let the hunters get away, but I will not leave those poor innocents here to be raped and slaughtered!" We waited until the hunters were far enough away and I leapt from the tree, landing in front of the men. I watched as the horror reached their faces. I proclaimed, "You were wrong, there are vampires and I am one!" They screamed and took off running. I heard Camaz leap from the tree. He was going after the two men that had gone to the left. I went after the other two. I reached for the dagger on my right arm and threw it at one of the men. He hit the ground hard. I leaped, landing on the back of the other man. I slammed him face first into the dirt. He was fighting me with all within him. But it was of no use. I flipped him over and straddled him. I unfurled my wings and watched as the fear rose in his eyes. By then my blood lust was fully ignited. I slammed his head to one side and struck. I felt his evil blood begin to flow into my mouth, setting my soul on fire. I listened as his heart took it's final beat. I raised up from my meal and went over to where the other man had went down from my dagger. His body was already growing cold. Then I heard the sweet voice of my beloved. He was on his way back to me. Once he arrived we took off for the castle to retrieve our other weapons. We alerted Devil of the hunters and for him to go to Cristos, to get the elite. They met us in the great field right outside the entrance to our cavern. While we were in our quarters dressing for the battle, I felt my hatred begin to build. Camaz came up and said, "I want you to stay close to me, my love. Do not leave my side for anything. I will not lose you to these hunters!" I promised him I would stay close and we left to meet up with our elite squad. We knew the scent of the hunters, so we had the others follow us. Soon we arrived at the hunters encampment. I pointed up to a tall tree, letting Camaz know I would be up there with my crossbow and I would take out as many as I could. I leapt to the top of the tree, placed myself on a large branch and made ready to start firing. I counted six in all outside of their compound. I knew I would only be able to take the first four out, before I have to reload. The other hunters would have just enough time to warn everyone else before I could fire again. I aimed my bow and let the four arrows fly, striking the four men in the chest. I watched as they fell to the ground dead. I quickly reloaded my bow and readied to fire again. But the other two men were already screaming for help. I watched as hundreds of hunters came running out of the compound. I let the next four arrows fly and reloaded, firing until I had ran out of arrows. I dropped my crossbow and took to the air. I pulled my sword from behind and swooped down, taking the heads of the first two hunters I encountered. I was quickly at Camaz's side. We began to battle the hunters. I caught sight of a hunter, readying his bow to fire at us. I leaped into the air, pulled my dagger and threw it at the man, striking him in the chest. He fell to the ground dead. I then came back down into the heat of the battle. Just as I landed I felt something strike my right wing. I screamed out in pain and looked, there was a dagger embedded in the wing. The damage was preventing me from taking to the air again. I pulled the dagger from my wing and pulled them within me. Camaz asked if I was alright. I told him yes, but my wing had been injured. But I would be fine. I reached for my two spare daggers in my boots and placed them on my arms. We took off after the other hunters. Suddenly one of them jumped me, knocking me to the ground. I watched as the hunter raised his sword. But Camaz was quickly on the man, tearing him to pieces. Camaz reached, helping me to my feet. Soon the battle was over and all of the hunters were dead. But some of our elite had been killed or wounded. We gathered up all of the wounded, taking them back to our headquarters. Then we went back for our dead. To my horror Stantos laid dead with an arrow in his chest. I cried for our good friend. The blood tears began to fall. I unsheathed my sword and raised it to honor our fallen friend. I swore on his lifeless body we would not rest until we had destroyed all hunters. Camaz picked up his lifeless body and leapt into the air, carrying our dear friend back to the compound. All of our fallen friends were honored at their funerals. Afterward we began our search and destroy mission to eradicate all hunters from the face of the Earth once again. My hatred for the hunters had ignited the heat within my heart and the hunters had better make ready, for Death's Deliverer was coming!

FROM THE AUTHOR

I hope you have enjoyed the continuing story of Anne and Camaz. I promise in book 4 things are really going to heat up for Anne. She will battle the beast within her and the Devil himself. You will meet new and fantastic creatures who become some of Anne's greatest warriors and friends. Will she ever defeat the devil and win her soul back? Below is a preview of the next book JOURNEY INTO DARKNESS.

CHAPTER 1

THE HUNT BEGINS

It had been three months since we lost our good friend Stantos. We had put his right hand man Sam in charge of our vampire elite. He was doing a wonderful job, but no one could replace Stantos in our hearts. We were in Chile in search of the hunters. We had wiped them all out in Mexico. Once we had cleared all hunters from South America we were heading to the United States. My wing had healed quite nicely over the last few months and I was able to fly with them again. As we searched the towns for hunters, we come upon a group of vampires. But those vampires were not like us. Their eyes were crimson red from the blood of the innocent. I could still remember the strength of Rose when she knocked me out. I became very frightened. Camaz saw the fear in my eyes and said, "Do not worry, my queen. All vampires are my children and I am their god. They must obey me." I watched as my beloved changed into his true form. He roared out to the vampires. I watched as all of them knelt to Camaz. He announced, "My children, rise, I am here to ask for your help in our war against the vampire hunters. Will you help your god?" They all stood up, cheering for my beloved. We then took off in search of the hunters. About an hour later I picked up on their scent. I pointed off to the west and we all took off running. We soon reached the encampment. There were hundreds of hunters there. I whistled for the dogs. They came up and sat down beside of me. I told them my plan and they were to go into the camp to distract the hunters and we would attack. I watched as my mighty Achilles and BamBam trotted into the camp. Some of the hunters came out and started to pet them. Soon most of the hunters had came out to see the dogs. I was high up in a tree with my crossbow aimed. I let the first set of arrows fly and reloaded, taking out four more. Now the entire camp was in shock. They spotted me in the tree just as I released another set of arrows.

They screamed out for their archers. I watched as four men came running out of a tent. Drew their bows and readied to fire on me. I thought to myself, "Oh, shit, didn't expect that!" I watched as they released their arrows at me. I heard Camaz scream out for me to get out of there. I dropped my crossbow and leapt into the air, unfurling my wings. The arrows just missed me but the hunters were reading to fire on me again. So I did the only thing I could think of. I let the fire in my heart begin to build and I caught on fire. The fire was burning so hot when the arrows hit me they melted. I reached behind me, bringing my sword around. It was blazing with the fire. I swooped down on the hunters like the mighty phoenix. I landed on the ground and raced at them. My speed was so fast all they could see was fire. I burned anyone near me. I spotted my love, in the battle of his life. There were three hunters and they were all trying to take him down. I reached down deep within me, pulled the fire from my heart and released it from my body. I watched as the fire engulfed all of the hunters. But the fire had taken everything out of me. I dropped to the ground and I was unable to move. I watched as the final five hunters ran toward me. I thought, "Oh god, I am going to die!" I cried out my beloved's name as they surrounded me. I watched as one of the hunters raised his sword, reading for the killing blow. I closed my eyes and whispered, "I love you, my mighty Camazotz!"